Damn, he shouldn't have kissed her.

Should have left well enough alone—especially since they'd come to an understanding. But the urge... Well, he'd hoped it would be quelled. It wasn't, though. Didn't even come close to it. In fact, one kiss had whetted his appetite. He wanted more. But he knew the result of that, didn't he?

Dear Reader

Welcome to the second book in my **New York Hospital Heartthrobs** trilogy. In the first story, THE DOCTOR'S REASON TO STAY, I introduced you to Rafe Corbett, who came home to meet the love of his life. In this story, FIREFIGHTER WITH A FROZEN HEART, you'll meet his brother Jess, who resists love at all costs.

When I first learned I was going to write these books, I knew instantly that I wanted a theme about the place to which we are all connected—home. But I wanted more than that. I wanted to write stories about what compels people to want to go home, and what binds their hearts to that special place. In this group of stories it was the love of a generous woman who touched countless lives...a woman much like your own mother, grandmother or aunt.

Cherished memories...that's what home is to me—and that's what home becomes for the heroes and heroines of **New York Hospital Heartthrobs**. Of course, going home isn't always the easiest thing to do. Just ask Jess Corbett. He lives large, and a little on the wild side. Home makes him restless, and all he wants to do is get away from it. But enter his childhood sweetheart: Julie Clark. It was love at first sight seventeen years ago, yet they were kids, and their youthful fling was cut short. Now he's home and she's back—and some of the old memories just won't leave him alone. Jess isn't going to get involved, though. But every time he turns around Julie's there, distracting him, reminding him that home with the right person can be good. So can he hold out against the temptation? Or will he give in?

I hope you enjoy Jess and Julie's discoveries in FIREFIGHTER WITH A FROZEN HEART. Then please come back to see what Dr Rick Navarro and Nurse Summer Adair are up to in my next **Heartthrobs** story. And, as always, I love hearing from you—so please feel free to e-mail me at Dianne@DianneDrake.com

Wishing you health and happiness.

Dianne

FIREFIGHTER WITH A FROZEN HEART

BY
DIANNE DRAKE

First published in Great Britain 2011
by Mills & Boon, an imprint of Harlequin (UK) Limited.
Large Print edition 2012
Harlequin (UK) Limited, Eton House,
18-24 Paradise Road, Richmond, Surrey TW9 1SR

© Dianne Despain 2011

ISBN: 978 0 263 22447 4

Harlequin (UK) policy is to use papers that are natural, renewable and recyclable products and made from wood grown in sustainable forests. The logging and manufacturing process conform to the legal environmental regulations of the country of origin.

Printed and bound in Great Britain
by CPI Antony Rowe, Chippenham, Wiltshire

Now that her children have left home, **Dianne Drake** is finally finding the time to do some of the things she adores—gardening, cooking, reading, shopping for antiques. Her absolute passion in life, however, is adopting abandoned and abused animals. Right now Dianne and her husband Joel have a little menagerie of three dogs and two cats, but that's always subject to change. A former symphony orchestra member, Dianne now attends the symphony as a spectator several times a month and, when time permits, takes in an occasional football, basketball or hockey game.

Recent titles by the same author:

THE DOCTOR'S REASON TO STAY**
FROM BROODING BOSS TO ADORING DAD
THE BABY WHO STOLE THE DOCTOR'S HEART*
CHRISTMAS MIRACLE: A FAMILY*
HIS MOTHERLESS LITTLE TWINS*
NEWBORN NEEDS A DAD*

**New York Hospital Heartthrobs*
Mountain Village Hospital

**These books are also available in eBook format
from www.millsandboon.co.uk**

**A new trilogy from
Dianne Drake:**

NEW YORK HOSPITAL HEARTTHROBS

Three gorgeous guys return home to upstate
New York. It's a place they love to hate—
until they each find a bride amidst the bustle
of a very special hospital.

With THE DOCTOR'S REASON TO STAY,
Dianne Drake welcomed you to
the first story in her trilogy.

Now, with FIREFIGHTER WITH A
FROZEN HEART, we see doctor
turned daredevil firefighter Jess Corbett
face his biggest challenge yet…

DEDICATION

**I would like to dedicate this book to
Julie Rowe, one of my best friends in the
world and the feistiest redhead I know!**

CHAPTER ONE

"IT's not your call, Corbett. You took in a lungful of smoke, so you go to the hospital to get checked out. Not my idea, not my rule either, but you do it, or you take a suspension." Captain Steve Halstrom folded his arms across his chest, looking properly stern in his edict. "You don't have a choice in the matter."

Jess didn't need to go, though. He didn't have a damn thing wrong with him. Wasn't coughing. Okay, so he'd broken enough rules for the day. He got it, this was the punishment. Meaning he'd have to leave his buddies behind at the scene, feel guilty as hell walking away from them while they were still fighting the worst of the blaze, just so he could pay the so-called piper. If his years as an army surgeon had taught him one thing, it was the value of working as a team. Today, against his better judgment, that team ethic would prevail, and he'd be sidelined. Do the deed, do the time.

He'd done the deed, couldn't argue the point… *much.* "Even though I'm a doctor, and I know—"

"What you know is that it's policy. You take in smoke, you take a ride to the hospital."

Jess looked up at the building—a three-story apartment, fully engaged. Everybody had got out, and that was the good news. The bad news was the wind, and the old building sitting so close to the one on fire that its demise was likely.

"Damn, this is lousy timing," Jess muttered, shrugging out of his turnouts—personal protective gear that was turned inside out when not in use so that the firefighter could quickly step into them and pull them on. A hundred pounds of heavy was what they called it, and it was a far sight different from the surgical scrubs and occasional lab coat he had worn when he'd been a surgeon. But that was just part of the career trade-off. He was okay with it most days.

Today, when he'd pulled that child out of the burning apartment and carried him down the stairs, letting him breathe *his* air, he'd been very okay with it. The child had been hiding in the back of an old closet. Couldn't be seen from a normal vantage point. Parents nowhere to be found. But one elderly lady had mentioned there might be a child up there, and that's all it had taken to raise the hair on the back of his neck. Granted, he hadn't known if the kid was still in there, but that hadn't stopped him. Not when there had been a possibility. "If I check out okay, I'm coming back," he told Steve.

"If you check out okay, you get three days off. This was a close one, Jess, and you brought it on yourself. So, you're on leave, *not suspension,* and if you argue with me, it'll be a week. Got it?"

"After what the lady told me, I should have just left the kid in there?" Jess snapped at his supervisor, instantly regretting it.

"You know what? Doesn't matter how you check out medically, take the whole week so you'll have plenty of time to think. Oh, and in case you've forgotten protocol, let me remind you that you are *required* to let someone know where you go. It's not an option. We don't do this job alone." He shrugged. "I don't want to have to hang you up like this, Corbett, but it's all I can do. This time you're off the hook easy. Next time I'll do something official."

Steve was right about this. Jess knew it. Didn't

have to like it, but he did know it. So now he had a whole empty week ahead of him. That, if nothing else, was his demon to deal with. "Then I'll see you in a week."

"Next week," Steve said, waving Jess off to the ambulance where *he* waved off the paramedic who tried to help him in.

"I'm fine," he grunted at her. Sitting out on the job, the way he was being forced to do, didn't square with him. But, different from the days when he had been head of trauma in the army, he wasn't head of anything now. Just another one of the many. Actually, one of the nearly fifteen thousand New York City firefighters and paramedics. One who was close to the bottom of the ladder. It was a good way to get lost, which was all he wanted. Get lost, stay lost. Do his job. Forget the rest of it.

"Which is why you're in my ambulance?" she asked, following him in the door. "Because you're fine?"

"Look, just do what you have to do, skip the comments and leave me the hell alone. Okay?" Plopping down on the stretcher inside the ambulance, Jess closed his eyes, even though the light was dimmed to almost total darkness. All he wanted to do was shut out the extraneous noises, but he couldn't. In Afghanistan, there'd always been noise…screaming, crying, artillery going off. Here, the sounds weren't the same, but they all amounted to suffering. Here, though, he got there first, made a *different* difference. Then he moved on, no commitments left behind.

"Too bad. The comments are the best part," she quipped.

Nice voice. A little throaty, which wasn't bad in the feminine variety…if he'd been looking for the feminine variety in anything. Which he wasn't. So he laid his right forearm over his forehead, not so much because it was a comfortable position but more to shut out what he'd see when his eyes adjusted to the dark. The equipment, the storage bins, the paramedic…not his life anymore. "Then comment away, *after* you check me out and release me," he said, not wanting to be a grouch about it. She was, after all, just doing her job, and being tough on her because of it wasn't his style.

"Well, it says here you took in some significant smoke, which means you get a free ride to the hospital like it or not. So, for starters, I need to put the oxygen mask on you…"

Now he was annoyed. He didn't need oxygen. Didn't want the damn mask clamped down on his face.

"No, thanks," he said, finally opening his eyes and shifting his arm up just enough to have a look when his eyes adjusted enough to make out a blur. First sight, red hair. Spunky red, even in the dimness. Short, boyish, in a pixie sort of a way. "Skip the oxygen. My lungs are fine, no matter what my captain thinks."

She moved toward him, carrying both an oxygen mask and a blood-pressure cuff.

"Blood pressure's okay, too. Unless you put that oxygen mask on me."

She laughed. "Scared of a mask, fireman? A little bit claustrophobic?"

"Not scared or claustrophobic. Just don't need it," he said, now wishing he could get a better look at her. He was pretty sure she was shapely. Nice curves in silhouette. Oddly familiar to him, even in the dim light.

"Says you?"

"Says me. I'm a…used to be a trauma surgeon."

"I'm impressed, fireman. But not swayed. You get the mask, I get your blood pressure. And I don't negotiate."

"But do you compromise?"

"Whoa, the fireman has an offer to make?"

He couldn't help but chuckle at that. His paramedic was downright stubborn, and he liked it. "Not an offer. A compromise. I'll cooperate unconditionally when you take my blood pressure if you let me wear a cannula instead of a mask." Prongs up the nose were better than a mask any day. The thing was, when he geared up to go on a run, he was all about masks and other equipment. But a simple, lightweight, green oxygen mask…that was his last memory of Donna. Garbled words she'd tried saying to him through her oxygen mask. Words he'd wanted to understand but couldn't. Words he should have heard if not for that mask.

"So, fireman, are you always this uncooperative?"

"Only when I have to be."

"Let me guess. In your opinion, that's most of the time."

He chuckled. "You've got some bedside manner, paramedic."

"I try." She pulled the cannula from the drawer and handed it to him. "Since you seem to know my job, you do the honors while I crank this baby up to full squeeze." She was referring to the blood-pressure cuff she was dangling over him.

Damn, he really wanted a better look at her. She was tweaking his memory and all he could see right now were big protective eye goggles and a surgical mask. Smart move, considering all the soot and debris flying around out there, but very frustrating. "Is that a threat?"

"A promise." She took his blood pressure then tossed the cuff back in the drawer.

"One twenty over eighty. Pretty good, for a man in your disgruntled and extremely dirty condition. Here, let me clean some of that soot off your face." Grabbing a bottle of sterile water, she twisted off the lid then soaked a gauze pad and started to dab at his face. But he caught her wrist and stopped her.

"One twenty over eighty? Did you mean to tell me it was a *perfect* blood-pressure reading rather than just a pretty good one? Oh, and the dirty face is fine, it comes with the job."

She wrestled out of his grip. "And the fireman gets a demerit for the worst manners I've met all day."

"What the fireman wants is to get the hell out of here and get back to work."

"Like I said before, you get a trip to the E.R. After that, you're out of my hands." She gave a pound on the glass between her and the driver, indicating they were good to go, then handed him the wet rag. "Wash your face. I don't want you getting soot in your eyes. And no arguments, okay? I just want to get this over with. You're my last patient on my last run as a paramedic, and I don't want any hassles. Think you can manage that for me, fireman?"

"And I suppose you expect me to smile, too?" he asked, half cracking that smile.

"What I expect is that I'm going to do the paperwork now, and you're going to answer my questions. Smiling is optional." Sitting down on a fixed bench across from him, she picked up the clipboard, clicked her pen and wrote the date on her transport form. "Do you have a name?" she asked.

"It's Jess. Jess Corbett." He thought he heard a little gasp from her.

"Okay, *Jess*." She twisted until her back was almost to him, as the ambulance lurched forward, then lowered her mask and pulled off her goggles. "So, tell me, how did you end up here?"

"Kid trapped in a closet. I gave him my oxygen. My captain wasn't happy that I didn't go in with backup. You know, same old story." Now, this was frustrating. He thought she looked like… no, couldn't be. Voice was different. Hair much shorter. Curves more filled out. Julie had been a couple pounds shy of skinny, with long straight hair. Thin voice. Pretty, not gorgeous. But his paramedic, what he could see of her, was gorgeous.

"I mean *here,* in New York City, fighting fires. How did that happen?"

"That's on the paperwork?"

"No, but getting to know my patients gives me a better sense of what's going on with them. As in, are you always so grumpy or is this a reaction to your smoke inhalation?"

"Trust me, it's a reaction to my smoke inhalation, but not the kind of reaction you think it is." But she could be Julie. Except, Aunt Grace had told him Julie was working in the south. "In answer to your question, though, let's just say that I got tired of my old job, quit it and decided to try something new."

"Well, I suppose quitting is good...*for some people,* isn't it? You know. As in running away."

Julie! He sat up, swung his legs over the side of the stretcher and yanked off his oxygen cannula. "I thought you were working down south someplace."

She turned to face him, full on. "This is south, compared to Lilly Lake." She reached up, switched on the bright overhead so he could see everything. "Julie Clark, R.N., paramedic." Said in all bitterness.

Well, this was certainly awkward. His first love. His first...everything. It was so awkward he didn't know what to do. Bail out of a moving ambulance, lie back down, shut his eyes then pretend she wasn't there? Let her have it out with him before they got to the hospital? Which was long overdue, actually.

With the way her eyes were sparking now—the same beautiful blue eyes that kept nothing hidden—jumping from the ambulance seemed like the best way out of this mess…for him. But he'd been the one who'd laid out that mess back then, and running away a second time sure didn't feel like the honorable thing to do. Hadn't then, didn't now. So, Jess gritted his teeth for the confrontation, and since this was Julie, he knew there would be one. Being feisty had always been part of her charm, and he didn't expect any of that had changed.

"It's locked," she said, as if sensing his thoughts. "You're not going anywhere."

Was that a barbed smile crossing her lips? "So, what's the protocol here, Julie? Do I ask how you've been? Should we sit here in silence and stare at each other? Or would it be easier if you beat the hell out of me and just got it over with?"

"If I weren't on the job, I might just take you up on that one. But since I am, here's an idea. How about you be a nice, cooperative patient and lie back down, and I'll be the paramedic who watches your vital signs and makes sure you don't go into respiratory arrest as some aftereffect of the smoke inhalation? Does that work for you, Jess?"

"Are you going to put a pillow over my face and smother me?"

"Is that what you want me to do? Because I can."

"Look, Julie…"

She shook her head, and thrust out her hand to stop him. "Lie down. Now! And don't argue with me."

"Sure," he said, doing just that. "And I suppose if you really want me to wear a mask…"

Julie laughed, but it had a cutting twinge to it. "Jess Corbett, trying to comply. It doesn't become you, Jess. Not at all. Besides, I'd rather watch you lie there and be uncomfortable around me. Good show, watching you squirm."

He did stay down for about a minute, hating every blasted inch of silent space around him. Then he popped back up. "You said I'm your last patient. Does that mean you're quitting?"

"Moving on. Went to nursing school part time for years, all the way through to my doctorate, and now I'm going to work as a full-time nurse."

"Congratulations," he said, still pretty much at

a loss for words. It wasn't every day that you ran into a childhood sweetheart, one he'd actually had feelings for. Of course, he'd made fast work of that. But, still, Julie… She *was* a memory-maker. Gone from his life, but never forgotten. "Well, I hope you have a good career. Aunt Grace would have been proud of you." What a lame thing to say, but he really couldn't think of anything else except, maybe, to apologize. After all this time, though, that seemed so trite, and under these circumstances so contrived.

"Oh, I intend to. So now, unless you have a medical concern or question, be quiet. Okay? I don't want to talk to you anymore. Don't want to listen to you either."

Too bad, because he liked the sassiness in her. He'd liked it seventeen years ago, and it hadn't changed much. But once they dropped him off at the hospital, that was going to be the end of the line for Julie and him…*again.* It was for the best, he thought as he sank back down on the stretcher, shut his eyes and tried to blank her out. Definitely for the best.

"Signing out for the last time," Julie said, handing in her badge. This was it. After so many grueling years in the back of an ambulance, she was finally moving on to the place she'd always wanted to be. And it was a good move, being a nurse. Grace Corbett had helped her, had made everything possible. Had dreamed the dream with her. She sighed, thinking about Grace, missing Grace. "And glad to be moving on."

"Well, you take care of yourself. It's not going to be the same without you around here, Julie," her supervisor, a tall, big-boned woman named Gert, said, giving her a hug.

Good times, good memories, being a paramedic. Better ones ahead of her, though. *She hoped.* And two hours later, when she was tossing the last of her few incidentals into a cardboard box, she was still looking forward, not backward, because looking backward would be filled with thoughts and memories of Jess Corbett…the last person she'd ever expected to find in the back of her ambulance tonight.

Jess…darn! Now she'd opened the floodgates, and he'd poured through in a huge way. The funny thing was, she didn't try holding him back. In fact, she shut her eyes for a moment and indulged herself. Jess… He was bigger than he was last time she'd seen him. More muscled. Lean. Fit. Broader shoulders. Face more chiseled, edgier lines to it. His eyes, though...still the same sapphire blue, but harder. Much harder than she remembered. No laugh lines around them either, which made her wonder if he ever smiled. His hair was the same, though. Sandy, maybe a little darker than it had been seventeen years ago. Clipped a whole lot shorter than she'd ever seen it on him. She liked the stubble on him, too. Made him look...masculine. Not that Jess, as a teenager, hadn't been masculine. But Jess *then* compared to Jess *now*...actually, there was no comparison. Jess the man and Jess the boy, the man won hands down.

"But I'm not going to think about him," she said, heading down three flights of stairs, grappling with the last of the things she was taking to her new life. She had an emergency room to expand. New responsibilities to think about. And thinking about Jess distracted her. So she wouldn't. That's all there was to it. She would not think about Jess Corbett.

An hour later, as she turned onto the interstate taking her north, she was still trying not to think about him. Of course, this new life she'd chosen for herself wasn't going to make that easy, was it? Not when her destination was Lilly Lake, and Lilly Lake was the place they'd almost started a life together.

For early spring, the evening was pleasantly warm. Tonight, the sun was setting in gold hues over the lake, and in the distance the wail of a loon saddened the expanse. Heard for miles, across land, and from lake to lake, it was the haunting call of mates looking for each other, mates lost to each other and calling out to find them. Jess knew what that was about, what it felt like to search. "So that's the long, sad story of my exile from New York City."

"Smoke inhalation?" Rafe Corbett snorted a laugh. "They grounded you a week for smoke inhalation?"

"*Two* weeks," Jess grumbled, then chuckled. "Let's just say that I overstepped my bounds. After my clean bill of health I shot off my mouth when I should have kept it closed, and my captain decided to put me on ice for a little longer to think about it."

"In other words, you don't play by the rules."

"And you do?"

"Okay, so the Corbett men do things their own way. But for me, that's fine. I'm an orthopedist, I don't really have to get into much of the team spirit the way you do."

An orthopedist who, not so long ago, hadn't been all that different from Jess. Except now Rafe was a married man with a daughter, and another one on the way. The picture of perfect contentment, and happy to be in that place. "Well, team is where it's at. And between us, big brother, I do have some problems with that. I'm more used to…"

"Doing it on your own?"

Jess winced. It was true. He was a loner in most aspects of his life. In fact, he could probably count on one hand the number of times he and Rafe had actually sat down and talked as brothers these past dozen or so years. "Yep, doing it on my own. But I get the team concept, realize how important it is, even if I get ahead of myself sometimes."

"Get ahead of yourself? You ran into a burning building without telling anybody you were going in. That's a hell of a lot more than getting ahead of yourself, Jess."

"You're going to give me a lecture, too?" he asked, clearly annoyed, not with Rafe so much as with himself. He'd been wrong. He'd admitted it. But there was something inside him…something he just couldn't control at times. Sometimes he had to act, consequences be damned. "Because I've already heard it, and now I have two weeks to reflect on the *error* of my ways."

Rafe held up his hands in mock surrender. "Then it's over, okay? Not another word. So, do you want to come stay up at Gracie House? We've got better accommodations. Molly would love having her favorite uncle there to play with." Six-year-old Molly was Rafe's new daughter and part of his newfound contentment.

"No. The cabin's fine. But tell Molly she'll be seeing enough of me over the next couple of weeks that she'll probably get sick of me." In truth, he liked the cabin. Liked its rustic charm. A mile from nowhere, with just enough amenities to call it modern, it kept him isolated. What more could he want? "Tell Edie, though, I appreciate the offer, and that I wouldn't mind stopping in a couple of times for a good home-cooked meal if she's up to it. I don't want to put her out, though, considering…"

"She's pregnant, working until her due date if she can and she loves to cook. How about tomorrow night? That'll give her the chance to plan it, and give you the chance to settle in."

"You can do that, just make plans for your wife like that?"

Rafe chuckled. "Hell, no. But Edie didn't figure you'd stay at the house with us, so she told me to invite you over tomorrow night for dinner."

"And you're just trying to score points with me, making me think it was your idea."

"I need some points, because I've got a favor to ask you."

"Sounds ominous."

"Not ominous. More like a matter of practicality. And to be honest, I'm glad you're home because I was going to come to the city next week to talk to you about it."

Jess twisted in his seat. Was on the verge of getting up and going inside. Shutting the door on what Rafe was here to discuss. "Another time?" he asked, trying to put off the talk for no good reason other than he didn't want to deal with it at present. In fact, his preference would be signing his share of Lilly Hospital over to Rafe, then be done with the whole thing. But that's not what Rafe wanted. So Jess was hanging on, but in title only.

"Look, Jess. I understand it's hard for you, and if there was any other way to do this, I would. But we are co-owners…"

"One of which who wants nothing to do with the hospital. So, here's what you can do, Rafe. Anything. *Anything* you want. I trust your judgment, and I'll give you my blessing but, please, leave me the hell out of the decisions. Okay?"

"What I want, Jess, is to take Rick Navarro on as a partner. He's earned it. He deserves it. And he has good ideas for expansion…"

Jess waved him off. "What, in the definition of *anything* don't you understand?"

"For once, just listen to me, okay? Before you start spouting off your opinion or telling me all the reasons you don't give a damn, just shut up and listen!"

Jess huffed out an impatient sigh. "Do I have a choice?"

"You've always got a choice, but I was hoping you'd give me some support in this."

"You've got my support, Rafe. Just not my attention." He pushed himself up out of his seat and headed toward the front door, but stopped before going inside. Change of heart? Not at all. But a sure change of mind. Rafe was the only person he had in this world, and it wouldn't hurt him to listen to his big brother. After all, Rafe had taken the beatings for him, quite literally. All those years, all the tirades, Rafe was the one who'd stood up to their old man and taken the punishment. So at the least he owed him another minute to listen. "Okay, tell me, but don't expect anything from me other than listening. Because I'm not going to get involved in this."

Rafe stood, and went to lean on the banister across from the front door. "Fine. I'll make it fast. We're expanding pediatric services, which you already know. We're looking into some growth in obstetrics, too. But the first thing we're taking on is an expansion to our emergency services, because what we have isn't good enough."

At the mention of emergency services, Jess winced. Being a former trauma surgeon, this was probably where Rafe wanted to wheedle some kind of commitment out of him. *Come back and work temporarily until we can find someone else to take over. Or be a consultant.* That's what he expected, but he was going to hold his ground. No involvement, no way!

"Rather than sending major trauma cases to the hospital all the way over in Jasper, or someplace even farther away, we're going to expand enough to handle what we need and help with overflow from other areas. So we've hired a nurse-coordinator to oversee the first phase of growth. She has an amazing trauma background, a doctorate in nursing…"

"A doctorate?" he asked, feeling his gut churn.

"A doctorate. And for where we are right now, she's the perfect person to put in charge of coordinating the plans. Um, Jess…we hired…"

"Let me guess. You hired Julie Clark?" He hadn't seen her in seventeen years, now here she was, front and center, twice in two days. How could that be happening?

Rafe frowned. "Either that was an amazing wild guess, or you've been in touch with Julie."

"In touch. *Not* by choice."

"Anything you want to talk about?" Rafe asked.

Jess shook his head. Didn't reply, so Rafe continued, "Well, she was the right one. Has the credentials we need, as well as the experience..." He paused, studied Jess's frown, sucked in a deep breath. "Look, Jess, since you're not here most of the time, and when you are you never leave the cabin, I didn't think it would matter."

"Why *would* it matter?" Jess snapped, then stormed inside his cabin and slammed the screen door behind him.

"Jess?" Rafe called after him.

"Nothing matters," Jess yelled back. "Not one damned thing." Except for those couple of weeks of Julie's pregnancy scare hell. Those had mattered a lot.

CHAPTER TWO

"I's strange being back after all this time," Julie said, dropping down into the chair across from Edie Corbett's desk. "I have good memories of Lilly Lake, and I appreciate all the help you've been, helping me get settled here again."

"I was new in town just about a year ago, so I know what it's like trying to get yourself established, even if you did live here before."

"It wasn't for long…just a few years, but let's just call them my formative years. And I really do want to thank you for letting me take a tour of Gracie House the other day. I didn't mean to just stop on your doorstep and beg to be let in, but…" Julie smiled fondly. "But I couldn't help myself. I needed a few minutes to come home."

"And you're welcome to *come home* any time you like. Our doors are always open."

"I'll bet I'm not the first."

Edie laughed. "As a matter of fact, no, you're

not. Several of Grace's children have stopped in, and Gracie House seems to be a focal point in their lives. For me, it's interesting to meet the people who've passed through her life…and her doors." She glanced fondly at a picture of Molly, her new daughter, and Grace's former ward. "Interesting and life-changing."

"Well, I spent the most important years of my life there. I was kind of a wild child, all my various adoptive parents threw me out, I had nowhere to go other than the juvenile home, and Grace stepped in and offered to take me. She made the difference, and it wasn't always easy for her, dealing with me. But she had so much…"

"Patience?" Edie asked.

"That. But I think it was faith. She never saw the bad side or the difficulty in people. Whatever the situation, she always managed to turn it into something positive. Like the time I stole a couple hundred dollars from her and took a bus ride to New York City. I don't think I really intended on running away so much as exploring the world, but the minute I stepped off that bus, aged sixteen, it was like all my small-town ways just wanted to pull me back. I was scared to death.

Didn't have enough money left for a decent meal. Nowhere to go. No one to help me. I mean, I was overwhelmed, and not as smart as I thought I was. So I called Grace, and she said she'd come get me. And she wasn't angry, Edie. In fact, she told me it would take a few hours for her to get there, so I might as well wander around, see the sights while I could. She even suggested a couple places I should go. *Julie, take advantage of your adventure*...that's what she told me. And when she finally picked me up, she asked me if I'd had a nice day. A nice day? I was expecting the wrath of God to fall down on me, and instead she took me to a very swanky restaurant, we spent the night in a glamorous hotel and the next morning she actually took me shopping. Then, when we got home, she asked me if I'd learned my lesson. To be honest, it took me a while to figure out what it was because to a crazy sixteen-year-old, it seemed like I'd been rewarded for my so-called crime."

"So, what was the lesson?"

"To trust and rely on the people who love you when you have a problem. That they won't let you down if you give them the chance to help. She told me if I'd have let her know how I was feeling, told her how much I wanted to go to the city, she could have taken me. But I didn't give her that chance because I figured she would say no. I didn't trust her enough to be honest with her." Julie laughed. "A mistake I never made again. Oh, and she did require a little extra work from me in the stables to pay her back for the money I took…work in the form of a shovel and pitchfork. Which, actually, is why I'm here. I was wondering if the foundation could use an extra volunteer. I loved working with the horses when I was a teenager. I think that's probably what grounded me more than anything else…being the person trusted with the care of another life. It certainly made me find things in myself I didn't know were there. So now that I'm back—"

"Always!" Edie interrupted. "It seems like the more horses we take in, the further our reputation spreads. Rafe's in the process of coordinating the building of another stable, one for the more critical horses. Sort of like an intensive care, I think. And we're renovating both the old stables, enlarging them and modernizing the facilities. So we can use all the help we can get, and then some."

"Well, I can still shovel..."

"There's plenty of that to be done. And lots of other things, if you decide that shoveling isn't quite the exciting time you remember."

"Never exciting, definitely not the thing I wanted to be doing, but it was quite a character builder. Of course, Grace knew that when she put me on the task. And I'm not too proud to do that again, or anything else you need. I have a lot to pay back, and with the way Grace loved her horses..." A stray tear slid down Julie's cheek. "Working with Grace's horses again is one of the biggest reasons I applied for the job here in Lilly Lake. I'd just hoped to be doing it with Grace."

"I miss her, too. And I didn't know her for very long. But she made such an impact on my life in such a short time...brought me together with my husband, gave me my daughter. I owe her everything."

"Me, too," Julie whispered reverently. "Everything."

On the verge of tears herself, Edie cleared her throat. "Well, then, why don't you stop over this afternoon, after you get off work, and have a look at the horses we have right now? I'll let Johnny Redmond know you're coming, and I'm sure he'll have some details and schedules for you to go over by then. Oh, and I'd love to have you stay for dinner, if you don't have other plans. It's spaghetti night at Gracie House. Nothing fancy. But it's Molly's favorite meal, so please, join us if you can."

"I'd love to, if it won't be an imposition."

"No imposition. But bring an appetite. Molly helps cook, and let's just say she cooks *big*."

"Then I'll see you later on, with a big appetite," Julie said, standing to leave. "So, if I may ask, when are you due?"

Edie instinctively laid her hand on her belly. "Another month. A little girl. Do you have any children?" she asked.

"No. Never been married, never been a mom. I'm more of the career type, I think."

"I was the career type, too, and look at me now." She glanced again at Molly's picture, then the one of the three of them—her, Rafe and Molly. "I'm into family in a huge way, and loving every minute of it. It's everything I *never* knew

I wanted," Edie said, laughing. "And I wouldn't have my life any other way."

There was a time she'd thought that, too. But then she'd been a kid with enormous, romantic delusions. Luckily, she'd grown up. A little of it the hard way, maybe. She'd learned her lessons well, though, in large part thanks to Grace Corbett. "Well, I'd better get back to work. So I'll see you later, Edie," she said from the hall. Turning, she hurried back to the emergency department, where she was responsible for more things than she'd ever thought she'd be responsible for. Thanks, in part, to Grace Corbett, too. Actually, thanks in full, since it was Grace's benevolence that had made paramedic training first, then nursing school afterward, possible.

"Looks like we're feeding an army tonight," Jess commented on his way into the dining room. The spaghetti bowl in the center of the kitchen table was heaped to overflowing, and the bread plate had enough garlic bread piled on to feed half the population of Lilly Lake. It reminded him of coming home to Aunt Grace for a meal.

"Uncle Jess!" Molly squealed, launching herself

into his arms with such a force it nearly toppled him over backward. "I've been waiting for you to come visit us. I have a new pony...actually, I have two ponies now. Lucky, my old pony, and she's not really that old. Johnny says she's about two, so that really makes her my new pony, since Snowflake, my new pony, is really about six, which makes her my old pony."

"Whoa, slow down," Jess said, laughing. "You're talking too fast, and I can't keep up. So, your old pony has a new pony, and Lucky Snowflake is who?" he teased.

"Lucky is my pony, and so is Snowflake, silly," Molly replied.

"Oh, now I get it. You have two ponies. Lucky is one, Snowflake Silly is the other."

"Not Snowflake Silly," she said. "His name is Snowflake."

"Didn't you tell me his name was Snowflake Silly? I'm positive that's what I heard." He looked at Rafe for support. "Isn't that what she said? Snowflake Silly?"

Rafe smiled, threw his hands into the air in surrender and backed away. "I'm leaving this one up to you two while I go help my lovely wife toss the salad." With that, he backed all the way into the kitchen, stopping short of Edie, who was wielding a large butcher's knife, going at the lettuce with a vengeance. "It really is a lot of food," he commented offhandedly.

"I invited someone else this evening," she said, eyeing a big, juicy red tomato for her next chopping chore. "Someone from the hospital."

"Anybody I know?"

"Maybe. She's fairly new on staff. Very nice. Originally from Lilly Lake, so you might know her. Her name's Julie Clark."

Rafe, who had picked up a carrot to munch, nearly choked. "Well, this ought to be interesting."

"How so?"

"Julie and Jess have history."

"What kind of history?"

"Big history." He patted his wife's belly.

"You're kidding. They were…?"

He shook his head. "False alarm. But it had us all going for a while."

"So, what should we do? I don't want either of them being uncomfortable. Especially not Jess, with everything he's been through—a war, the death of his fiancée, a career change."

Rafe gave his wife an affectionate kiss on the cheek. "Well, I'm sure eating spaghetti with a former girlfriend will shrink in comparison to all that."

"You may be a great doctor, but you're not so smart about relationships, are you?"

"I get ours right, don't I?"

"You get ours perfect. But we don't have history…torrid history."

"I didn't say it was torrid."

"No, but…" She patted her own belly. "That sure implies it, don't you think? Anyway, he's here and Julie's down at the stable, talking to Johnny, so she'll be up in a few minutes. And you, my dear husband, are in charge of dealing with the situation."

Rafe shrugged, then gave over to a smile. "Like I said, could be interesting. Jess needs something to shake him up, and Julie might be it."

"What might be it?" Jess asked from the doorway.

"This might be it," Edie hedged, holding up

her butcher knife. "The best one I own. This one might be...*it.*"

Jess gave them both a half smile. "Domesticity has really dulled you two down, hasn't it?" he asked. "So much ado about a knife?"

"Hey, little brother. Believe me when I tell you there's nothing dull in this house. In fact, I think you're about to find out just how un-dull Gracie House is going to be."

"What's that supposed to mean?"

"Me, Jess. I think Rafe's referring to the two of us having dinner together." Julie looked at Edie. "Molly let me in, by the way. Hope that was okay? Oh, and I brought non-alcoholic sparkling grape juice. Knew you couldn't do wine, but I thought this might go well with the spaghetti." She held the two bottles out to Edie, but Jess was the one who took them and marched straight to the refrigerator on the other side of the room—as far away from Julie as anyone in the kitchen could get without opening the back door and continuing on into the yard.

"Thank you. So, I take it you and Jess remember each other?" Edie asked, with a sly wink at Rafe.

"Actually, we had the chance to catch up with each other just a few days ago…in New York," Julie said. She was clearly not as uncomfortable as Jess was at this meeting. If anything, she was almost too noncommittal. Trying too hard to stay unaffected. "In the back of my ambulance. He was my very last patient as a paramedic."

"So, that's how it was. Jess was your patient." He arched an amused eyebrow at his brother. "Bet he wasn't a very good one, was he?"

"No, he wasn't."

"Did you have to strap him down?"

"Do you two realize I'm standing right here?" Jess cut in.

"Sure we do, little brother. But since you're not contributing to the conversation—"

"Look," Julie interrupted. "It's clear I'm the outsider here. How about I take a rain check for another night? That way Jess will be able to enjoy the lovely meal Edie has prepared without getting tied up in knots having me sitting on the opposite side of the table from him."

"If anyone should leave, it's me," Jess said. "You're the guest, I'm just the—"

"You're both overreacting," Edie broke in. "This is a meal. A simple meal. That's all. Food, conversation…don't read anything else into it. Molly's excited, having both of you come to dinner, and we're not going to disappoint her. So, Jess, have a seat at the table. Julie, sit anywhere you'd like. Rafe, go tell Molly dinner's ready." She sucked in a deep breath, then dropped down into one of the kitchen chairs. "Oh, and in case you didn't notice, we're eating in here tonight. I didn't want to make it formal by setting the dining room. So relax, be casual." She smiled sweetly. "Sit with your backs to each other, if you must. But let me warn you. I have a ton of food, and neither of you is going anywhere until that spaghetti platter is clean."

Julie laughed. "I think I can manage my fair share, in spite of Jess being here."

"Ditto," Jess grumbled.

"Do you two want some time to air some dirty laundry before we eat?" Edie asked. "Because you're welcome to use the den."

"No laundry, dirty or otherwise," Jess said, taking his place at the table.

Julie took her spot diagonally across from Jess. "None at all. Not one single, solitary piece of it."

"Why don't I believe you?"

* * *

"So I suppose now's the time to ask," Jess said. He'd followed Julie halfway to her car, trying to decide what to do. Truth was, he didn't know what was proper here. They'd made it through dinner, kept the conversation light enough. But those sideways glances he'd caught her giving him…no mistaking her feelings. Now here they were, ex-lovers, ex-friends—Jess wasn't even sure what they were—standing six feet apart in the driveway on a starless night where the moon didn't even have the decency to exit its cloud cover, both of them so stiff they wouldn't have even swayed in a wind squall.

"Ask what?"

"Several things, I think. First, how are you?"

"After all these years, that's the best you can do?"

"Okay, let me try something else. How have you been getting along?"

"You mean, how have I been getting along *without you?* Is that what you want to know?"

"Okay, stupid question. Let me try again."

"There's nothing to try, Jess. If there were, you would have tried it, or said it, the other day in the ambulance. But you didn't."

"Because you told me to shut up."

Julie shook her head. "Look, let me make this easy on you. I live in Lilly Lake now, work at the hospital *you* own, and that may put us into close proximity from time to time. Which means we need to learn how to deal with…us. What we were, what we weren't."

"What we were, Julie, were kids, doing the things kids do."

"Not all kids do what we did. I mean, I'm assuming you're not forgetting…"

"No, I'm not forgetting. Believe me, I've thought about us, about what happened, over and over all these years. Thought about how it could have turned out differently, where we might be now, if it had. The thing is, I'm not that same person, Julie. I've lived a lifetime since then, had regrets you can't even begin to imagine, and all I can say to you right now is that I'm sorry. I was a stupid, thoughtless kid. I should have trusted you more. But I didn't. I said some bad things and I am sorry."

"So am I," she said, her voice flat. "Sorry you thought I was trying to trap you, but I'm also sorry I didn't tell you the truth sooner than I did.

And that I didn't get to apologize. But you left me, Jess. You walked away from me and never gave me the chance."

Jess shut his eyes, heaved out a heavy sigh. "You were sixteen, Julie. I was seventeen. We really didn't have a lot of choices. And you didn't have anything to apologize for." He opened his eyes to look at her, but she had turned away from him, staring at her car. "There really wasn't a right or a wrong way to get through it, and I suppose all either one of us can say about it now is that we did the best we could."

"Or maybe there was a better way, and we just didn't take enough time to figure it out. Anyway, you said you're not the same person you were back then, and I'm certainly not the same person I was, so let's just not dwell on the things we messed up. Okay? I have a good life going. A great life, thanks to your aunt. She was everything to me, Jess, and because of that, I don't want to fight with you. So can we agree to be cordial with each other?" She truly wanted to add *not looking back* to that request, but she had looked back, more than once over the years, and she always would. Because there'd been a few days when she'd dreamed of being a wife and mother. Those dreams had made her happy, probably the happiest she'd ever been because she'd been in love with Jess. Totally, completely in love. With the qualifier that it had been the love of a rather immature sixteen-year-old. With a baby on the way... Or so she'd thought until the test had come back negative.

The dream had come and gone so quickly. It had taken her some time to come to terms with it, come to terms with the end of her future fantasy life, but the day she'd gone to tell Jess the truth... She still had nightmares. What she'd done to him, the pain she'd caused him...

Her pain, too. But she'd thrown herself into making a better life. And succeeded. Which was why she was surprised by her feelings now. Surprised by the pain that was slipping its way back in. Seeing Jess again was good, but it hurt.

"Cordial is good," Jess agreed. "I'm not expecting anything. Don't deserve anything. And, God knows, you've got every right to hate me. What I did was inexcusable."

"No, it wasn't. Like you said, we were kids." Kids who never got a chance to be kids. Maybe that's why their emotions had been so intense. At such young ages, they'd both known so much pain. "Anyway, it doesn't matter now. But I'm curious. Did Grace ever know I thought I was pregnant? Did you ever tell her?"

Jess shook his head. "I never told her, but she probably knew anyway. That's how she was."

Yes, that's how she had been. "Well, that was around the same time she started talking to me about making *real* plans for my life, trying to show me some options for finding a better way. Anyway… I need to get going. I'm heading back in to work the night shift in a little while, and I'd like to run home and grab a quick shower first. So… I'm glad you're feeling better after that incident in New York. And I'm really glad you have such a good family here to take care of you while you're recovering. You're a lucky man."

"Well, I'll be here next week for spaghetti night, and I'm sure my family would love to have you come back, if you can. So maybe I'll see you around…"

"Maybe," she said, heading for her car. Although she wasn't sure she wanted to. Or wasn't sure if she could. Because right now her head was spinning and her chest hurt. All she wanted to do was get into her car, drive away and go someplace where she could cry for the things that had never been, and the things that never could be. All of them about Jess.

Puttering his way along the back road, Jess wasn't in any particular hurry to return to his cabin. It wasn't that he minded being alone. That's the way he spent most of his life now. In many ways, it was preferable. Getting involved, having someone be the center of his life…what was the point? As much as he'd loved Donna, he hadn't been able to make the real commitment to her, the one every future bride should expect from the man she'd consented to marry. He'd tried. Gotten involved in the plans, smiled when she'd talked about the dream. *Their dream.* But she'd known he'd been struggling with all that…permanence. Had asked him about it, even though he'd denied it. Yet it had been something he hadn't been able to hide, and the closer they'd got to that permanence, the more it had shown on him. Then he'd hurt her and for that he'd never forgive himself. She'd loved him and in return he'd broken her heart.

Was that what she'd been thinking about when she was killed—her broken heart, his inability to be everything she deserved?

Even now, two years after Donna's death, there wasn't a day that went by when he didn't replay those last few moments with her. Could he have done something different? Been different for her? Maybe faked the feelings? Faked the whole *happy with the domestic lifestyle* thing until he had settled in and it had become a habit?

Donna Ingram. Beautiful. Smart. Full of life. She'd always led with her heart and, in so many ways, he envied that. All she'd wanted had been a normal life with a man who'd never had normal in his life. Impossible odds, as it had turned out. And overwhelming regrets.

Tonight Donna was on his mind, as she often was. Tonight, though, Julie Clark was also on his mind, but for other reasons. Julie had been his first love and, once upon a time, they'd made plans, too. Sure, their plans had been childish. They'd talked about running away together. Or maybe getting jobs and saving their money so

DIANNE DRAKE 51

they could backpack or bike across America, or Canada, or the whole of Europe. Impractical plans that had seemed so real and so exciting for a short time. But then Julie had thought she was pregnant, and, stupid kid that he was, he'd been thrown for a big curve. So he'd taken the easy way out by listening to his dad. *It's a trap, Jess. That's all it is. She's setting a trap for you. So, don't be stupid, son. Kick her to the curb before it's too late, before she ruins your life.* Yeah, great advice from a drunk child abuser and overall mean slimeball of a man who'd masqueraded as the town doctor. The hell of it was, he'd listened. He'd accused, he kicked, then he'd run. What a jerk!

But that was only the first time. He'd pretty much done the same thing with Donna, hadn't he? Maybe not kicking her to the curb so much as edging her there. Being gentle, trying not to hurt her in the process. But it was all the same and, in the end, he'd hurt her anyway.

Now, tonight, an entire lifetime of miserable failures was poking him from every side, and he just wasn't in the mood to be poked alone. So, turning off the main road, Jess headed back to

Lilly Lake. Brassard's Pub was as good place as any to be in a bad mood. He didn't drink, didn't smoke, didn't care to play darts. But he craved the noise. Wanted it all around him. Wanted it to permeate every pore in his body, reminding him that he was still alive since he wasn't even so sure about that. So, yes, Brassard's was the place. Loud jukebox, louder bartender, and on a good night, a crowd that could be heard halfway over to the next county. Yes, it was exactly where he wanted to be.

"Jess!" the bartender yelled across the noisy room. The owner-bartender, Will Brassard, was also head of the Lilly Lake Volunteer Fire Department. "I heard you inhaled."

Jess thought about waving him off in favor of an isolated corner, but Will was a nice guy, married to a nice woman, father of some nice kids. Living the life Jess had thought he'd have by now. "Twice," he shouted back. "I inhaled *twice.*"

"So what did they give you for it?" Will shouted. "A commendation?"

If only… "Two weeks *vacation.*" Rather than shouting the story, which he knew he was about to tell, he shoved his way through the crowd, half of them dancing to the music, and made his way to the bar stool on the end, the one where he didn't have to sit and face himself in the mirror behind the bar. "Two long, restful weeks up at the cabin, looking at the walls, pacing the floor and taking up knitting because...let's just say that I didn't follow orders as well I should have. Funny how that works out, isn't it?"

Laughing, Will held out his hand in greeting. "Well, my wife knits, and it's not all it's cracked up to be, because if you don't follow the knitting rules, you end up getting...well, to me it looks like a big ball of knots. So, if you're looking for some activity..." He pointed to the far end of the room, where several of the locals were engaged in what seemed to be a rather bland card game... one eye on the cards, one eye on the old, large-screen, rear-projector TV where reruns of a college basketball game were wobbling across the screen in hues of green and orange.

"Not my thing, but thanks for the offer. Likewise, don't do darts."

Will started to point to the beer tap, but stopped. "That's right. You don't drink either, do you?"

"Because I'm boring as hell. I work and I sleep.

And when I get back to Lilly Lake, I don't even do that much."

"So, why are you here tonight? You've been coming back home off and on for a year now, and I don't think you've ever been in here. In fact, other than passing you on the road a time or two, this is the first time I've seen you, period."

He genuinely liked Will. They'd known each other in school. Not too well, but well enough to know that the boy Will Brassard had turned into a good man. "It seemed like a good place to stop, and since I was in a stopping mood…"

"Coffee?" Will offered. "Or a soft drink?"

"Coffee's good."

"And let me guess. You'd rather have it over there at the table in the corner, so you don't have to put up with me talking to you, or asking questions."

"Actually, that was my intent when I came in here. But I think I'll stay at the bar, if you don't mind a non-drinker taking up a perfectly good drinking spot."

Will laughed. "Any firefighter is welcome at my bar, for any reason, any time. No matter what they're *not* drinking. Stay as long as you like."

It was a friendly invitation, and Jess appreciated it. But by the time he'd polished off his third cup of coffee, he was restless again. Even the noise and activity weren't enough tonight. Problem was, he wasn't sure what was. No point in staying here, though. Not when the night was young and someone paying for more than a cup of coffee might want his seat. So Jess dropped a generous tip in the tip jar, saluted his farewell to Will, and headed for the door. But before he got there, a shout above the crowd stopped him.

"We've got a run, Jess. Grease fire in the kitchen, out at the lodge. Care to join us?"

Jess's heart lurched. Did he care to join them? Hell, yes, he cared. In fact, the adrenalin was already pumping.

"May have a couple of minor casualties we have to run into the emergency room," Will responded. "How about you being our medic on this run?"

Hadn't Julie said she was working Emergency tonight? Suddenly, he wanted to see her again. He wasn't sure why, and didn't have time to think about it as Will tossed his bartender apron to one of the waitresses and leaped over the bar. So maybe this wasn't going to be a bad *vacation,* after all. At least, not this part of it.

CHAPTER THREE

"IS EVERYBODY out?" Will Brassard shouted across the ruckus of firefighters struggling to get through the line of bystanders watching the flames shooting out the kitchen roof. Set against the backdrop of the black night, the orange glow was an astounding work of art, mesmerizing its watchers, stalling them in place, causing congestion in the area. Also, the hundred or so patrons evacuated from the restaurant, combined with the two hundred guests at the lodge hotel and various guest cabins who were leaving by a sundry of exits, were causing quite a commotion, some in shock, some confused, some simply looking for a safe place to go. Consequently, by the time the Lilly Lake volunteer firefighters had arrived and readied their equipment to face down the fire, about a third of the population of Lilly Lake was either there, or on their way to watch the show.

"Not yet!" one of the volunteers practically

screamed at the top of her lungs. "I think we've got three more people still in the kitchen, doing God only knows what. Manager of the lodge says they're trying to account for everybody registered right now, and they'll let us know in a minute if we've got to worry about that."

"Like we have a minute," Jess snorted. He was suited up and heading in through the cluster of people. Not thrilled, though, to be called to paramedic duty. Of course, Will probably thought he was a natural, maybe even assumed that's what he did in the city. But it wasn't. He shunned medicine now. Yet here he was, carting medical equipment through a crush of gawkers, getting ready to do something he didn't want to do. Except there was no way he could turn his back on these people. No way to tell Will he wouldn't do it. It wasn't in him. Wasn't like him to turn his back. Probably one of the few good character traits in him, thanks to Aunt Grace. "So, where are the injuries? And do we know what we have so far?"

"We've got them in a couple of places. The less serious injuries are out back in the caretaker's cottage," Will shouted. "We have a couple of more serious ones going to the third guest cabin down from the pool. Decided to put them there because transport out will be easier, and we're clearing the parking lot and road in right now for the ambulances. Got five coming in, by the way. The one from here has an ETA of less than five minutes, and the other four coming in from Jasper and Hutchings are still twenty to thirty minutes out. And, Jess…one of my men just radioed, and we've got what looks to be a bad injury on the way down. Burns, maybe something else cardiac. They couldn't tell, but he's going in and out of consciousness."

"Okay." Jess took a harder grip on the medical kit Will had thrust at him once he'd climbed out of Will's SUV. Serious injuries, one ambulance in town and the possibility of a long response time. "What about a helicopter, if we need it?"

"We can get one, but time out on that's going to be forty-five minutes, if we're lucky." Will was running hard to keep pace with Jess. "Give me the word, and I'll get it ordered."

"So that's all we've got in the way of transportation?" It wasn't good enough and, frankly, he was surprised he hadn't known the status. But what did he know about anything concerning the medical or emergency needs in Lilly Lake?

"Well, we can get them into the hospital here pretty fast, but until the expansion on the emergency department begins, they're limited in what they can do."

Which frustrated the hell out of Jess. He wanted, no, he'd always *demanded* immediate response and the best facilities, yet he owned a hospital that wasn't yet ready to offer what he would demand…if he still practiced as a doctor. He needed to talk to Rafe about it, see what they could do to fix it, in a hurry. Back away from his plans to *not* get involved and get involved in this one thing. "But the hospital's ready to receive, what? The less serious injuries?"

"It's ready to receive whatever we send them. They're a good bunch there, and they'll do whatever they can to get those we can't keep out to facilities that can handle them. So, don't worry about that end of it. It'll work." The voice answering wasn't that of Will, though. It was Julie, and she was following on Jess's heels, running just as hard toward the guest cabin as he was.

"What are you doing here?" he shouted at her.

"Came to help. Like I said, I've got everything well covered at the hospital, got staff that came back in the minute they heard about the fire, so Rick...*Dr. Navarro*...asked me to come out to the field and coordinate efforts here. They do that in Lilly Lake, send hospital personnel out when there's a need."

A klatsch of women too busy watching to notice the rescue operation in progress swarmed over the path leading to the guest cottages, essentially swallowing up the passageway. Jess swerved to avoid them, but Julie pushed her way right through. "Look, ladies, you're going to have to move back," she said, stopping for a moment. "All the way to the other side of the building."

"Anything we can do?" one of the women asked.

"As a matter of fact..." Julie motioned them closer to her. "We've got a lot of personnel coming through here now, with more on the way. Maybe you ladies could keep the area clear for me, make sure people stay back, sort of take control of the pedestrian traffic flow."

Jess smiled, hearing the words. She was, essentially, turning part of the problem into the solution. Smart gal. Natural leader. He admired that.

"I didn't know you were so resourceful," he said, once she caught back up to him.

"I was living on the street when Grace took me in. You get to be very resourceful when you don't have a roof over your head or a meal in your belly."

Apparently, there were a lot of things about Julie he didn't know. "I guess I never knew that either." What, exactly, had he known about her back then, other than she'd attracted him like crazy? He thought about it for a moment, and came up with nothing.

"Nobody knew. I didn't want anybody's pity, and Grace was respectful that way, not telling anyone."

That, she had been. And he missed her more and more each day. "She was," he agreed, still fixed on the image of Julie being homeless. He'd been young, but how could he have not known?

Arriving at the guest cabin where the more serious of injuries were being brought, Jess was first in the door. Greeted by several volunteers, townspeople who all stepped away when he strode in, he looked first at the log rail bed in the corner of the room where a middle-aged man was being attended by a woman still clad in her black-and-white checkered chef pants and a white jacket. She was putting cold compresses on his head, and a second appraisal showed he was the only patient in there, so far. Meaning the bad one was still en route.

"Okay, I'm Jess Corbett," he said above the murmur of the bystanders. "Doctor...er, firefighter. So, what do we have here?"

"Chest pains," the woman said. "Shortness of breath. And he's looking a little...pale. His name is Frank Thomas, he's our head chef."

Jess was immediately at the bedside, taking the man's pulse. Rapid, thready. He was diaphoretic...sweating. Shortness of breath becoming pronounced.

"What do you need?" Julie asked, peering over Jess's shoulder.

"Get his blood pressure, get him on oxygen, then get an IV, normal saline, ready." He looked at Frank. "Frank," he said, assessing the man's responsiveness. "Are you allergic to anything?"

"Cats," Frank managed to whisper.

Jess laughed. "Well, then, I won't be treating you with any cats today. Any medicine allergies, or reactions you can recall?"

Frank shook his head.

"Good. I want you to take an aspirin for me." He looked around, saw Julie strapping the blood-pressure cuff to Frank's arm. "Anybody here got an aspirin?"

With that, three different people produced a variety of types, and Jess chose the low dose, then popped it into the man's mouth. "Chew it up, Frank, and swallow it."

The man did, with great difficulty. "Am I going to be okay, Doc?" he forced out.

Doc. It had been a long time since anybody had called him that. Strange how it sounded. Kind of nice, though. "We're doing our best, Frank. Right now, we're going to get you stabilized, then send you to the hospital, where they'll be able to run tests to see exactly what's going on."

"My wife," Frank gasped.

"I called her," Julie said, stepping up with an oxygen mask. "She's going to meet you in the emergency room." With that, Julie placed the mask on his face, then whispered to Jess, "It's low, ninety over sixty." After which she immediately set about the task of finding a vein in Frank's arm and inserting an IV catheter. "You're going to feel a little stick," she said, as the needle slid in as smooth as melted butter. She glanced over at Frank, saw that he didn't respond, not even a tiny flinch to being stuck, and she nudged Jess, who was busy hooking EKG leads to Frank's chest. "I think Frank, here, is on the verge of taking a little *nap*."

"Frank!" Jess shouted, giving him a little shake. "Wake up, can you hear me?"

Franks's eyes fluttered open.

"Do you have any history of heart disease?"

"No," he sputtered. "Healthy…"

"Ever had chest pains that you can remember?"

This time Frank didn't respond. Rather, he stared up at the ceiling.

"Come on, Frank," Julie said, slapping him on the wrist, trying to stimulate him back into paying attention. "Stay with us, okay? We need you to try hard and answer the questions Dr. Corbett is asking you. It's important."

Frank nodded, but didn't look away from the ceiling, and it appeared he was having difficulty even doing that. Jess gave a nod to Julie who, without asking, knew to get the defibrillator ready, just in case. She was impressive, taking his nonverbal cues, setting out drugs that might have to be administered, getting the endotracheal tube and laryngoscope ready. It's what she did in the normal course of her day, and what Jess used to do, too. But somehow, seeing Julie work the way she did knotted his gut. She was so…good. So confident. She'd gone so far beyond anything she'd ever thought she could be back in the days when she'd wanted him. Good for her, he thought. *She did better than anything I could have ever been for her.*

"Frank, you're having a cardiac episode…heart attack," Jess explained. "Are you on any kind of medication, for *any* condition?"

The man shook his head, a wobbly, feeble attempt at it, but the effort was more than he was able to endure, and his eyes dropped shut. "Damn," Jess snapped, immediately scrambling into assessment mode, trying to locate a pulse. Which he did, thankfully. "Weak," he said. "Respirations getting more shallow, quite a bit more labored, too." Meaning Frank was winding down.

"Julie, could you check his blood pressure again? I have an idea it's dropped."

She did, then tried a second time. "Not hearing it," she said, pumping up the blood-pressure cuff a third time, on this attempt feeling the pressure with her fingertips. "Palp at fifty," she finally said.

"So when can we get him transported?" The three or four minutes they'd been working on the man seemed like an eternity, and the thing was, in the field there was little or nothing they could do for him unless, God forbid, he crashed. Which was getting perilously close to being the case. But in even the most scantily equipped hospital, which he hoped *his* hospital was not, there was a world of options and miracles that would save Frank's life, once they got him through the door.

"Someone, check on transport," Julie shouted to the three or four people in the cabin who seemed to have no function other than wait. "Go find Will Brassard, the fire chief, and tell him we've got a patient we've got to get out of here right now!"

"Big voice," Jess commented, plowing through the kit containing the cardiac meds. He wanted something to kick-start the heart in case it decided to stop, and he found it in the form of a tiny vial of epinephrine. "Don't remember that on you before."

"That's because it's an acquired talent. I had to work on it. Bad patients in the back of my ambulance need a big voice sometimes. Patients like you were."

He chuckled. "So you took shouting lessons?"

"Something like that. Part of some assertiveness training Grace had me take."

"Money well spent," he said. "You're about as assertive as anybody I've ever known."

"In a good way?" she asked, taking the vial from Jess and drawing the liquid into a syringe, getting ready to act.

"In a good way." A very good way.

"They're ready to take him," one of the volunteers called from the door. "And they said to tell you they're bringing in a critical from the kitchen right now."

It was almost an amazing switch. As one Frank Thomas was carried out the door to the nearest ambulance, one Randolph O'Neal was rushed in and deposited in the very same bed Frank had just vacated. Only, right off the bat, both Jess and Julie saw the grim prognosis for the restaurant's sous chef. He was burned extensively on his legs, shoulders and chest, a combination of second- and third-degree burns. His breathing was raspy, gurgly. He wasn't conscious. He also had a gaping, bleeding head wound. "I need saline," Jess shouted, then looked at Julie. For a moment they exchanged knowing glances… glances that spoke volumes in the span of a fractured second.

"I'll get a helicopter in," Julie said.

Jess, already in assessment mode looking for pupillary reaction in the man, simply nodded, already seeing the bleak reality. Unfortunately, the bleakness was only confirmed when Jess pried open O'Neal's eyelids, flashed his penlight, saw fixed, dilated pupils. No reaction to light. "Nothing," he said, cursing under his breath and at the same time, strapping a blood-pressure cuff on Randolph's arm.

Julie didn't even bother asking what it was because, judging from the grim expression on Jess's face, it wasn't good.

"Oxygen, IV, saline for the burns..." he said, on a frustrated sigh. "You know the drill."

Julie immediately turned to the group of bystanders, all but one of whom had gone out the door when Randolph O'Neal had come in. "You got any kind of medic training?" she asked the boy, who appeared to be a busser at the restaurant.

"No, ma'am. Except I can do that squeeze thing if somebody's choking."

"Can you pour liquid over this man's burns?"

"Yes, ma'am. I can do that."

And just like that, Julie had recruited a volunteer who stepped forward to assume an important part of their patient's treatment.

"Got a broken leg," someone shouted from the door.

That someone turned out to be Rafe, who was leading the way for two firefighters carrying yet another patient on a stretcher.

"It's about time you showed up," Jess quipped.

"Well, I'll be damned. You're the medic in charge?" Rafe asked.

"I'm the medic in charge, which means you take the broken leg because..." He looked back at his patient. Didn't finish his sentence as Randolph O'Neal's breathing had just gone agonal…into near-death mode. Rafe must have seen the same thing, as he tried stepping between his brother and O'Neal.

"Look, you don't need this right now, okay? You take the guy we just brought in and I'll deal with this."

"Because I can't?" Jess snapped.

"Because you shouldn't." Rafe stepped up, took Jess by the arm, tried to move him. "Jess, his pupils are blown," Rafe whispered. "He's not going to make it. Not to a hospital, not anywhere."

"I don't give up on my patients, Rafe," Jess growled, bending down over the man.

"Jess," Julie said, laying a hand on his shoulder. "Rafe is right. We can't… There's nothing…"

A hush fell over the cabin as the inevitability became apparent to everybody there, and within seconds the cabin cleared of everybody but Jess, Julie, Rafe, the two patients and James Orser, the young man who was still, dutifully, dousing Randolph O'Neal's chest with saline, even as O'Neal exhaled his final breath.

Julie laid a hand on James's arm, whispered for him to stop. "Go sit with the patient who was just brought in," she said. "I'll be over there in a second." She looked at Rafe, whose agony for his brother showed in his face. Then she looked at Jess, who seemed…numb. "There wasn't anything we could do," Julie said to Jess, as Rafe went to treat Max Fletcher, the man with a compound leg fracture that had happened outside the lodge, well away from the fire…a bystander who'd come to watch and gotten in the way of a pick-up truck. "He was so badly injured, he wouldn't have made it to a trauma center, and even then…"

"I know," he said. He was a trauma surgeon, after all. Well, trauma surgeon, past tense. But he still had all the knowledge, still had the same feelings, present tense. And this was why he'd left medicine. It was too late. O'Neal had come to him too late. He had needed to be there sooner. And Jess had needed to be the first one to look, not the last one. All his years of medical training yet by virtue of being the surgeon he was always the last one in line. That's what he'd figured out on the battlefield. What he still knew. What he still hated.

Suddenly, nausea welled up in Jess like a water balloon stretched to its limits and ready to explode. Without saying a word to Julie, he ran outside, straight to the bushes and retched until there was nothing left inside him, then gave way to dry heaves after that.

"Leave him alone," Rafe said, stepping up to Julie, who was halfway to the tree line, running after Jess to help him. He grabbed her by the arm and forcibly stopped her.

"Why? Can't you see he needs help?"

"What he needs is to be alone, to work it out."

"He lost a patient, Rafe. He's taking it hard."

Rafe let go of her arm. "He lost a fiancée in Afghanistan. Almost two years ago now. And, yes, he's still taking it hard."

"Oh, my God," Julie whispered. "I didn't know."

"He doesn't really talk about it.

"I'm so sorry, Rafe." She turned to look at Jess, who'd finally straightened up. "That's why he left medicine? Did he lose heart?"

"I don't think he lost heart, or else he wouldn't

be out trying to save lives in a different way. To be honest, he's never told me what's going on with him. I've asked, but he shuts me up, tells me it's nobody's business."

"But you can't let him go through this alone right now, even if he thinks he wants to be alone. You know that's true. So which one of us going to go over there to see if he's okay?" she asked.

"That would be you, because I'm going into the hospital to operate on Max Fletcher's leg. Headed there right now. And, Julie, just so you'll know, Jess is as apt to push you away as he is let you in. Don't take it personally. Jess loved Donna and she died in his arms. I'm not sure how you get over something like that. Or if you can. But Jess is stubborn. He won't let anybody get too close, and you do know some of the reason for that."

She did. "Thanks for telling me about Donna."

She gave Rafe a squeeze on the arm, then went to Jess, but before she could say anything, Jess held his hands up in surrender. "I don't need help," he said. "I'm fine."

"You don't look fine," she said, handing over a bottle of water. "In fact, you look like hell."

He took the water, uncapped it, swished some

around in his mouth, then spat it out. "He told you, didn't he?" he said, wiping his mouth on his sleeve.

"Some. Not much. And I'm sorry, Jess. I didn't know."

"Well, it's not exactly captivating conversation." Taking one more swig, he rinsed and spat again, then capped the bottle. "So you see why I'm a firefighter now...the story of my shame. I don't do trauma so well."

"Not shame, Jess. A lot of other emotions, but not shame. And as for not doing trauma well, that's only your opinion. I saw you work in there, saw the way you took care of Frank Thomas and tried with—"

"Oh, so now you're being nice to me?" he interrupted. "Pity the man who's off vomiting in the woods and offer him some good-hearted words that you wouldn't have offered him an hour ago?"

"And you would have me do, what? Ignore someone who needs my help?"

"Who the hell told you I needed help?"

"It doesn't take a genius to see what you're going through, Jess. I just thought—"

"Don't. There's nothing here worth wasting

your thinking on. What I was, what I am now...
they don't connect, okay? Don't think you're
going to play the part of some little do-gooder
who's going to step in and make things right for
me, because it's not going to happen." He stepped
around Julie, appraised the scene. "Looks like
the fire is squared away. Why don't you go see
if there are any more injuries that need treating."

"Is that how it's going to be, Jess?"

"How what's going to be?"

She shook her head. As badly as she felt for
him, there really wasn't anything she could do
to help. Rafe had been right about that. Jess had
shut his brother out as masterfully as he was shutting her out. And if life had taught her one thing,
it was never to force herself into a place where
she wasn't wanted. Clearly, she wasn't wanted
here. Even so, her heart did break for Jess. She'd
loved him once. Had wanted to have his baby
once. And, apparently, she still had a few leftover
feelings for him. Feelings from the past, though.
Only from the past.

"You still here?" Julie asked Jess, looking up
from the desk she was slumped over, finishing

up the last of the paperwork from the injuries at the restaurant fire. In total, six treated in the emergency room and released, two admitted, one of them gone to the operating room and now in Recovery, one under cardiac observation but doing well. And one fatality.

"Just checking on Frank Thomas."

"He's resting easily. Dr. Navarro doesn't think he needs to go to a hospital with a cardiac care unit because, so far, the tests are showing that his heart attack was fairly minor."

"You look like you should be resting," Jess commented.

"I'm fine. I've worked longer and harder than this. And as soon as I put my signature on this last piece of paper, I'm out the door."

"Would you like to stop somewhere for a cup of coffee on your way home?"

Actually, all she wanted to do was go to bed, sleep hard, sleep long. Because she was scheduled to be back on duty much sooner than she wanted to be. But something in Jess's eyes, something in his voice, compelled her to accept his invitation. "Look, how about I meet you at the coffee shop down on Main Street in about twenty minutes?

I can't stay long, but a nice caramel mocha latte sounds good."

He chuckled. "I didn't figure you for the fancy stuff."

"A girl's got to have her indulgences, Jess. Caramel mocha latte happens to be one of mine."

"Then I'll have one waiting for you," he said, then turned away. But before he was away from her desk, he spun back to face her. "Look, Julie, about last night, and some of the things I said..."

She waved him off. "Just go get us a table and order the coffee, okay? The rest of it doesn't matter." Even though it really did. But she wasn't going to be the one to fix it for Jess. He didn't want it, and she couldn't afford the involvement. As long as she kept that in mind, she'd be fine.

"I ordered you a large," he said, a little while later, as she sat down across from him at the table located in the front window.

It was like they were on display, the ideal couple drinking coffee together that anyone strolling by would see. The perfect place, if you wanted a place that lacked intimacy. Which this table did. In a way, she was grateful for the public display, because that kept things honest. And with Jess, this time around, that's all she wanted. Honesty. "Thank you."

"And a blueberry muffin. You used to love blueberries, didn't you?"

"You remembered that?"

"Actually, I hadn't thought about it for years, but when I told the server that I was ordering the caramel mocha for you, she told me you usually get a blueberry muffin with that, so I ordered one. And that's when I remembered you loved blueberries."

For a moment, she was disappointed. Then she chided herself for having some stupid, romantic notion that, after all these years, he would have remembered something so trivial. Of course he wouldn't. Just like she wouldn't remember something trivial about him, like…like… "Do you still have an aversion to pepperoni on your pizza?"

He chuckled. "Still hate it with a passion. How'd you remember that?"

Truthfully, since that night when she'd treated him for smoke inhalation, she'd remembered a lot about Jess Corbett. Too many things, probably. "Don't know. I suppose it just came to me."

"Well, for what it's worth, my pizza taste has

gone to all veggies. Don't eat any meat on them nowadays." He took a sip of his chai tea. "Still don't like coffee either."

"That's a new one on me. But we were kids. I don't suppose we ever had the occasions to do coffee, did we?"

"Donna was the one…she used to tease me about my peculiar appetite. She drank probably ten cups of coffee a day, black, no sugar, no cream. Definitely no caramel."

"And you two served together?"

He nodded. Looked out the window, fixed his gaze on something in the street. "She was a medic. Damned good in the field." He cleared his throat. Blinked hard. "Look, I appreciate you trying to help me last night, and I apologize for being such an idiot about it. But that's my history, isn't it? Being an idiot at the most inopportune times."

"Well, we were young at that particular inopportune time. Different problems, different… ideals, I suppose. And history's just that…history. In the past. We learn from it and move on. Or hopefully learn and move on. No need to apologize for last night either. Rafe had warned me that you probably wanted to be alone, and I should have listened to him. But sometimes I'm headstrong, sometimes I go getting myself into situations where I don't belong, and what you were going through...I clearly didn't belong there. So it's me who should be apologizing to you for bothering you. But I truly am sorry for your loss, Jess. I blundered right in where I shouldn't have."

"It wasn't you, Julie. And whatever Rafe told you about how I push people away, he was right. I do. It's easier that way. You know how we were raised, Rafe and me...my old man. Even though I wasn't the one who got the beatings...I was there. Saw what he did to my brother. Wasn't able to do a thing to help Rafe. Wasn't able to do a thing to help..." He took a sip of his tea. "Anyway, enough of that. Let's talk about something more pleasant, like what a good nurse you are. I'm impressed. Not surprised, though, because you were always strong."

She smiled. "Well, I don't know about being strong so much. But I'll admit, sometimes it impresses me, too. Not that I'm a *good* nurse so much as that I am a nurse. It was my little-girl dream, the only one I ever had, really."

"You never wanted to be a fairy princess?"

She shook her head. "Always a nurse."

"But you were a paramedic? How did that happen?"

"It didn't take as long to get through the training as it did to study to be a nurse, and being a paramedic got me into the medical field while I was studying. A practical choice on my way to nursing, I think. And I'm nothing if not practical. Oh, and Grace figured into it, too."

Jess chuckled. "Why am I not surprised? She seemed to have a plan for everybody she loved, didn't she?"

"Grace…she expected something of me. No one ever had, but Grace always did, and when I messed up, which I did a lot, she didn't criticize. She just stood by me, showed me better ways. I think her offering me paramedic training was her way of testing my dedication to medicine, since I didn't really display much dedication for anything else, except the horses. She knew that side of me…the side where I acted first and thought about the consequences later. I was barely eighteen, and all I wanted to do was go to nursing school. I didn't think about all the years of education on a university level I'd need. My grades were so poor in high school I barely got out. And there I was, begging to embark on this long journey of even more education.

"Grace knew I wasn't ready for it. So I knocked around in odd jobs for a while. Then she offered me a shot at paramedic training. Less in the academic pursuit, more in practical experience. She was testing me, Jess, to see if I could do it. To see if I could dedicate myself enough to pass the first hurdle. Which I did, because I loved working with people who needed help...needed *my* help."

"But you still wanted to be a nurse?"

Julie nodded. "That never changed."

"So Aunt Grace eventually paid your way to nursing school?"

"No. Somewhere along the way, I figured out that getting through nursing school was something I had to do for myself. It would have been easier letting Grace support me all the way, which she would have done. But I didn't want easier. I wanted to earn my way in the world, which I did as a paramedic. Grace gave me my start, and helped me here and there when I needed it, but it was by her example more than her bank account that I found my way." Julie smiled fondly. "And it was hard, working my job full time and going to school. There were times I wanted to quit… or drop out for a semester or two. But Grace believed in me…the only one who ever did.

"I'm sorry I missed her funeral, but I had university exams and Grace wouldn't have wanted me to postpone. My thoughts were with your family that day, though."

He reached over and squeezed Julie's hand. "You're right. She would have definitely had an opinion about you missing your exams. A strong opinion!"

Julie brushed back a tear. "Look, I really need to get going. I have to be back on duty later, and some sleep between now and then would be a good thing." She pushed away from the table. "It was nice talking to you, Jess. When we were kids…well, that was different. *We* were different and we made a mess of things. But like I said, that's history. Maybe now we could be friends? I think Grace would have liked that." Funny, how easily that had come. All these years, all the harsh feelings…they didn't matter now. Because what she said was right. They *had* been kids. That's all. Just kids who hadn't been smart enough to know how to deal with their problems.

"I think she would have liked that," Jess said, standing.

Grace would have liked that. But Jess hadn't said he would. And that was disappointing. Bitterly disappointing.

CHAPTER FOUR

"SEEING anything interesting?" Julie walked over to Jess, who was leaning against the wall in E.R. Exam 3, and leaned next to him. It was near the end of her shift now and, good Lord, was she ready to go home! Between her normal duties, meeting with an architect to go over expansion plans *ad nauseam,* ordering E.R. supplies, conducting a brief E.R. staff meeting, interviewing one candidate for a full-time nursing position and fretting over the fact that Jess Corbett was simply hanging around, watching, she was wiped out. He'd been there over three hours now, hadn't really said much to anybody about anything, including her. More like he was an impressive, immovable presence standing off by himself in one spot or another, making her uneasy for reasons she didn't want to get into.

"Lots of things," he said, his voice so sharp it could have cracked glass.

"Anything I should know about?"

In answer, he shook his head. That's all. One shake of the head. Well, that wasn't what she'd expected from him. Somehow she'd hoped for friendly, or cordial, or even semi-sociable. "So, are you interested in a guided tour of the area...or something? There's probably not much that you haven't already seen, but maybe I could answer some questions or show you some of the ideas I'm working up for the expansion." She was pretty sure he wasn't interested or else he would have already said something. But he owned the place, and she felt obligated to try. More than that, she was worried about him.

"Appreciate the offer, but I know my way around. And, yes, I'd like to see your ideas."

Well, that was a step in the right direction. Twenty minutes later, when they were sitting together in the cafeteria, drinking coffee, and she was running through a list of things she absolutely needed to make the expansion successful, she was wondering if they were still going in the right direction because, as usual, Jess was rigid, all observation, no talk. "Space-wise, we could use more room," she pressed on, wishing he'd say something, make a noise, at least grunt. Which he hadn't done so far. "But the architect believes that in order to stay inside the basic footprint he's laid out, we're going to have to sacrifice a little of what I'd hoped for in order to keep the whole layout more efficient. Apparently, I'd planned too much wide open space he considered wasted."

Finally, something provoked him enough to speak. "Wide open space is wasted?" Jess broke his rigid posture by crossing one long leg over the other then leaning back in his chair. "Why's that?"

Julie shrugged. "I thought it would be nice to spread things out so people won't feel so cramped or claustrophobic when they're in here. But he said wasted space is wasted money. In other words, why build something that's not going to generate revenue?"

"Sometimes it's not about the money."

"Well, you and I might agree on that, but Mr. Masters has a good reputation for his medical facility designs and he's probably right."

"So you're just going to back down?"

"If I get what I want, Jess, something else has

got to give. If that happens, then I blow the budget I was given to make this work."

Jess drew in a deep breath, then let it out slowly. "Have you factored in a bigger ambulance bay?"

"What we have is fine."

"For one ambulance. But one isn't enough, which means that whole area is going to have to be expanded. And I want the doors from it leading straight into Emergency, rather than the way it is now, where the patient is offloaded and has to take a long trip down through what is, essentially, the administrative offices."

Julie raised her eyebrows, quite surprised to hear that Jess had actually thought this through. "Well, I'd actually come up with an idea to relocate the ambulance bay at the back and have admittance through a small triage area. You know, first assessments."

"But?"

"But budget."

"Yeah, well, it's not about the money. So I say to hell with the budget. Design your ideal, then we'll see what we can do. And in the meantime, I may toss in some ideas of my own." He pushed back his chair, then stood. And for the first time in hours finally cracked a smile. "You're not what I expected, Julie."

"What's that supposed to mean?"

"Back when we were kids, I think the thing about you that attracted me the most was your wild side. We were a lot alike in that respect. But what you've made of yourself... I know you give Aunt Grace all the credit, but the credit belongs to you, too. I guess I didn't think you could change so much because, in lot of ways, I haven't changed so much. Sometimes I'm still that teen-aged boy who's trying to figure it out."

"And sometimes I'm still that wild child who's just fighting to get through any way she can."

"Oh, you're getting through, Julie. I'm just glad that the hospital is reaping the benefits." With a nod of the head, he turned and exited the cafeteria, leaving Julie to wonder what that had been all about. Jess, getting involved in the expansion plans. Jess, being so complimentary.

It was nice of him. Strange, but nice. She liked it. Hoped she'd see it again because whether he recognized it or not, the Jess Corbett who'd just walked out of here had gotten through, too. Only thing was, he still hid from it.

"Julie…*Julie?*"

Somewhere in the distance someone was snapping fingers at her. Then Rick Navarro's voice shook her out of her thoughts. Much to her surprise, he was seated in the very same spot Jess had been, and she hadn't even seen him come up. "I'm sorry," she said, trying to click back to reality mode. "What was it you were saying?"

"I was just telling you to go home. You look tired. After last night, and with the day we've been having in Emergency, you need to get some rest. Doctor's orders."

She really liked Rick Navarro. As a hospital administrator, he was strong and fair. As a doctor, compassionate. As a person, he was just about as nice as anyone she'd ever met. She remembered him from when they were kids, although she'd never really had much to do with him. He was the son of Lawrence Corbett's maid. Had taken a lot of hard knocks from the kids at school because of it. It couldn't have been easy being the maid's kid when you were growing up in an affluent little town like Lilly Lake, and that was something she understood all too well. It hadn't been easy being the wild child either…the one all the parents had forbade their children from being friends with. Outcasts, both of them. A common bond. Maybe that's why she liked Rick so much. They shared similar history, and had come through rather well at the other end. It's probably the reason she'd jumped at his job offer, too. "I'm okay. Just a little distracted. Jess and I were just going over the expansion plans, and—"

"Jess?" He looked genuinely surprised.

"He has some ideas. Doesn't care if we go over budget either."

"Did you feel his forehead?" he asked.

"Why?"

"To see if he was burning up with fever. He's gotta be sick, delusional. The Jess Corbett we all know doesn't want to be involved here."

"Well, the Jess Corbett who was sitting in your seat only minutes ago got involved."

"Any idea why?"

Julie shook her head. "I think it might have something to do with last night. After Will Brassard called him out to work as a medic, I think he might have seen a different side of things."

"That can only be good. If Jess stays on this and we actually reap the benefits, I'll be happy."

"Then prepare to be happy. For what it's worth, I don't think Jess is going to back off." Said in all due tentativeness, though. She was pretty sure Jess meant what he said, the way he'd meant every word he'd said to her back when they'd been kids. The only question was, for how long? After all, he did have that history of running away. Yet he'd seemed genuinely interested in the expansion. Given that he didn't want to be here in Lilly Lake in the first place, though, she did wonder. "Anyway, I need to get back to work. I've got some papers to shuffle before I call it quits for the day."

"Paperwork can wait. You need to go home. You've already put in more hours than we allow, so I might have to get tough with you if you don't follow doctor's orders."

Julie laughed. "That's the best you can do for a threat? Where I come from, Navarro…actually, where you come from, too, you've got to back up those words with action."

"Like picking you up and physically removing you from the building?" He cracked a broad smile, arched playful eyebrows. "I can do it, if I have to."

"You, and what man's army?" She stood, though, glad to get the reprieve since she really did want to get out of there. Needed some space to breathe, to think…about Jess.

"Look, tough girl. Don't make me call Security on you."

"You know, it's good to be home. I really missed Lilly Lake, missed all my friends." Impulsively, she threw her arms around Rick and gave him a big hug. "Missed you, too, Navarro. So tell me, have you and Jess made up yet? Something outside the meet and greet and be cordial stage?"

Rick's expression sobered. "Rafe and I did when he came back. Jess is the tough one, though. He's keeping his distance."

"Well, Rafe told me about Jess's fiancée. I honestly didn't know anything about it." And she was a little hurt Jess hadn't been the one to tell her. "It's terrible, and I can't even begin to imagine what he's gone through, or is still going through. So I think he's having a hard time adjusting. I know I would. Also, I know, for a fact, he's not happy about having to take time off from work. But he brought some of that on himself."

"Brought it on being Jess?"

Being Jess. People who knew him knew exactly what that meant. "There is that side of him, isn't there?" she said, half smiling. In truth, that unpredictable side was part of what she'd found so exciting all those years ago. "And the problem is, *being Jess,* as we call it, has got him as many write-ups for taking what the fire department calls unnecessary risks as it has commendations for bravery."

"Grace worried about that. She was also pretty upset when he just up and quit medicine. Every time she tried talking to him about it, suggest that maybe he should keep some options open, he'd just shut her out." He shrugged. "God knows, I've had my share of trying to figure out where I want to be in life. Not sure I've got it all worked out yet, to be honest. So I know what Jess is going through."

"Well, right now he's pretty focused on the E.R. expansion, so I say we just take advantage of that and hope it works out as well for Jess as it will for the hospital." She meant that, too. She really did want it—whatever *it* was—to work out for Jess.

"And I think maybe I'll take the first *big*

step with Jess, and see what happens. I mean, I really don't have anything against him anymore. Making up with Rafe made me realize a lot of things about myself. The biggest, probably most important thing being that, as a father, I have to be an example to my son. Telling Christopher to do one thing and doing just the opposite isn't being that example."

Julie reached out and squeezed Rick's hand. "I'll bet you're just the greatest dad in the world. And I can't wait to meet Christopher. Anyway, as far as Jess is concerned, just give it a try and see what happens. He's a nice guy who really needs someone to reach out to him."

"Have *you* tried?" he asked.

Not enough. Sometimes the memories were too painful. Besides, what would happen if she did get through to him? They couldn't go back to being what they had been all those years ago and, for them, there was no going forward. So why bother? Actually, why even think about it? "Our history…" She shook her head. "He's not going to respond to me. I mean, professionally we can work together. That'll be fine. But I'm not the one who needs to be reaching out to him in any other way." Because it would hurt too much. As it was, she could hide behind her professional feelings when it came to Jess. That was easy to do. But she was discovering that her personal feelings were still raw. It was a surprise, after so many years, but there was nothing she could do about it except protect herself as best she could. Because this time, like last time, Jess would leave. Only this time she was forewarned. *Caveat emptor.* Let the buyer beware. Except she wasn't buying.

All the way home to change her clothes to go to the stables, and for the next hour after that, Julie wondered why she felt this overwhelming need to do something when she'd thought her recharged position on staying uninvolved was pretty clear. On the one hand, Jess was in a bad place right now, a place she'd been before. Half her life had been spent in a bad place, and if not for Grace Corbett…well, there was no telling how it would have turned out. Probably not as well as it had so far. Besides all that, Grace had done so much for her, and she wanted to give something back. Helping Jess… Grace would have liked that. Would have wanted it.

But could she stay away from him on an emotional level? That's what scared her. Not the history, not even the bad way they ended so much as the little twinges she felt, even now, when she thought about him. She remembered those twinges, remembered where they'd got her before. All those years ago, when the teenaged Julie Cark had encountered Jess Corbett for the first time, it had only been for a good time. That's all. That's who she'd been. But those twinges has sunk her. Done her in. Bowled her over when it had come to Jess. Which was what was making the so-called mature woman Julie Clark very nervous. In a life where she was pretty confident of herself at long last, this was one realm where she wasn't confident at all. So, in this whole debacle over what she wanted to do, could do, should do, literally any and everything after the next couple hours tending the horses was up for grabs. In other words, she had a great job and outside that, she was clueless, thanks largely to all this confusion surrounding her feelings for Jess.

One thing was certain, though. She did have to help him get through whatever was messing up his life. For Grace. Even for Jess. For herself, too, if she ever hoped to straighten out her own personal tumult.

"He's beautiful!" Julie exclaimed, standing on the opposite side of the stable, looking across at the gray Arabian Johnny Redmond, the stable manager, was showing off. "Except for the fact that he needs a few pounds on him, he's stunning." With its distinguishing head shape and lofty tail carriage, the Arabian was clearly one of the most aristocratic, most beautiful horse breeds in the world. At least, in Julie's opinion. It was a breed with speed, endurance and strong bones. Also, in her opinion, an Arabian stood out because of its good nature, its ability to learn quickly and, most of all, its willingness to please. Grace had often compared her to an Arabian, but she'd always known better. Those weren't her qualities. Far from it, in fact. But standing in the presence of those noble attributes, the way she was now, only solidified her conviction to help Jess. In her estimation, *he* was the one with the qualities of a good Arabian, even if those qualities were shrouded. "And he's got great spirit. It hasn't been broken. You can see it in his eyes." But there was distrust in those eyes, too. Or maybe just wariness from the abuses he'd suffered.

Again, she thought of Jess.

"You always did have a way with the horses," Johnny said. A retired jockey, Johnny was one of Grace Corbett's longtime employees, a vital part of the Gracie Foundation, where abandoned and abused horses were rescued, treated, brought back to health and adopted out, or given a home for life if adoption wasn't an option. Right now, Johnny looked after nearly a hundred horses, an odd assortment of mules, some donkeys and a small herd of wild, starving burros rescued from out West and relocated to Gracie Foundation's acreage. "Grace always hoped you would help run the foundation someday. Maybe now you'll get your chance."

Maybe she would. Although, it had been years since she'd had any good horse time. Coming back to it, though, and being entrusted with this stunning creature was just one more reason she was glad to be back. "Well, how about I start off slowly then work my way back into it, beginning with this handsome fellow?"

"That's what I had in mind for you, but you're

going to have to be careful. He's shy," Johnny
warned. "And he spooks easily. I'm also a little
worried that he's off his feed and, so far, we
haven't been able to get any substantial amount
of nourishment in him. Vet's been out to check
him a couple of times, doesn't see much wrong
physically except he's underweight and generally
weak. So if we can't get him to eat in the next
couple of days, we're going to have to force-feed
him, which I'd rather not do."

This poor creature had suffered too much pain
and anguish and, in a sense, turned himself into
a ghost. Like Jess, in some ways. But he still had
his spirit, the way she knew Jess still had his. It
was just a matter of getting to know that spirit
and nourishing it. "Does he have a name?"

"Normally, we let little Molly choose the
names. That's become her official role in the
Gracie Foundation, which is why our horses have
names such as Ice Cream, Licorice and Pretty
Girl. But we haven't let her in here with this one
because when we got him in, we weren't sure he
was going to make it and we didn't want Molly
exposed to something like that. She gets really
involved and there's no reason for her to see the

ugly side of how some people abuse these animals. So, no name."

"Then he's Ghazi, which is Arabic for conqueror, because he *will* conquer his abuses and be strong again. I see that in him." In Jess, too.

Johnny smiled in appreciation. "Then Ghazi it is. I'll go record it in the registry and, in the meantime, maybe you could take Ghazi out for a walk…if he'll walk with you. So far, he hasn't responded to anybody, but if you can get him out, the bonding experience would be good. For both of you. Also, he hasn't shown any mean tendencies, just skittishness, but I don't think he's ready to be mounted yet. So for now I think we should just lead him around the paddock then let him tell us when he's ready."

This horse deserved better than what he'd had before now, Julie thought. And soon he would get better. *She was sure of it.* "So, Ghazi," she said, approaching him directly, so not so spook him, "we're going to be friends, you and me. Best friends, if you'll let me."

The horse eyed her suspiciously, stepping back each time Julie stepped forward. But the stall was small, and he only took a few steps backward until he was trapped against the wall. She was instantly alerted, as this was when some horses would buck and rear. But not Ghazi, it seemed. He simply stood. Actually, he almost cowered, which made her wonder what could have happened to him to cause so much sadness. "I know I'm supposed to give you healthy foods like carrots, and Johnny would kill me if he knew what I was about to do, but do you like sugar cubes?" she asked, pulling a couple from her pocket and placing them in the palm of her hand. She got close enough that Ghazi could see the sugar, then let him make the next move, which was to move back toward her outstretched hand to take it. Risky business, if he decided to nip, but she didn't see meanness in his eyes. All she saw was sadness and fear...and so much spirit desperate to break through. "It's okay, sweetheart," she said in her gentlest of voices. "Whatever happened to you in your other life, it's never going to happen again. I promise you, you are safe here, and we love you. From now on, you're going to have the best life any horse could possibly have."

Because Ghazi was her horse now. She *would* adopt him. Beyond the shadow of any doubt, she

knew he was meant to be hers. Which meant Lilly
Lake had truly just become her home because
she had a horse here—a horse that needed her
care. No matter what else happened in life, she
was home to stay. Heaving a sigh of relief, Julie
swiped at the tears streaming down her cheeks.
Home…it had such a nice feel to it. So much
safety. It was good to be back. "Look, sweetheart, you need to make the first move. I know
that trusting me might not be easy yet, but this
is about you. So, please, just take the sugar." She
stretched out her hand to him just a little farther,
and this time Ghazi stretched his neck toward
her.

"That's good. Now, try to take one more step."

Which the horse did. Then so did Julie, happy
that she and Ghazi were making some kind of instant connection. It renewed her faith in her ability to judge horses. Hopefully, the same would
hold true for people. Namely, Jess. "Okay, baby.
Just a little closer." She extended the hand holding the sugar cubes just a little farther toward
Ghazi, then waited for his next move. Which was
another inching toward her. "Good, sweetheart.
Just keep coming."

Finally, when she was close enough to Ghazi to feel the moist exhalation from his nostrils on the palm of her hand, she took one final stretch and held herself steady there until the horse, at last, took the sugar cubes from her. She was pleased to find he was as gentle as a kitten, pulling back his lips and barely touching her flesh with his teeth. Ghazi was a mild-mannered soul, and she was totally, head over heels, in love with him.

"That was amazing, what you just did with him," Jess whispered.

Startled, Julie spun around. "How long have you been standing there, watching?"

"Almost from the beginning. Something about giving him sugar instead of carrots, and not telling Johnny, who by the way, in case you never knew, keeps a stash of sugar cubes hidden in his office, in his file cabinet, third drawer from the top."

"And you know that, how?"

Jess grinned. "Youthful inquisitiveness. Also knowing that Johnny is a creature of habit, and that some things never change. So, tell me about the horse."

"I called him Ghazi. And he has a kind soul," she said, not sure what else to say.

"So do you, Julie. You are going to keep him, aren't you? You were always partial to the Arabians, weren't you?"

"You remember that or did someone have to tell you, like they did the blueberry muffins?

"Actually, yes. I remembered."

"I'm flattered." Pleased as well. "And you liked the quarter horse, if I'm not mistaken." She smiled over a memory of Jess sitting astride his glorious palomino quarter horse, and her thinking he was the most handsome boy she'd ever seen in her life. Then the memory clouded, and her chest tightened. "Look, I've got to get back to work. I promised Johnny…" She stepped back. Tried turning away from him, but he grabbed her arm.

"I brought over some hospital plans for you to look at. Additions to what you've already done. I know we can't do this on a personal level, Julie. You make that clear every time you're around me, and I understand why even though you say you want to be friends with me, you can't. But we still have to deal with the hospital. And I don't want to make that tough on you." He should have just left the plans on the table by the door and gone. But he'd got himself caught up in the moment, watching her gentle up to the horse the way she had. It was a beautiful thing. Julie was a beautiful thing. She'd truly come home, and for a second he'd wished he could come home again. *Almost.* Then the reality had risen back up to bite him. He didn't have a home anymore. Not in any real sense. Didn't want one. Didn't need one. Julie's reaction to him only emphasized that.

"For the hospital," Julie said, then turned her back on him, pulled another two lumps of sugar from her pocket when Ghazi braved up enough to nudge her in the arm for it. "And it's not about not being friends, Jess," she said. "It's about so many things. Things I haven't figured out yet. Just give me some time, okay?"

"All the time you need." Because it didn't matter. He wasn't staying. She was. And she knew the score. Knew him. Watching Julie, all he could think about were the opportunities he'd missed along the way. His fault, every last one of them, so he couldn't complain. But, damn, he felt the sting anyway. And being here with Julie, it was more acute than he'd expected. More acute than he wanted because he knew...*dear God, he knew*...what he couldn't have even when he slipped up and let himself wish or hope or daydream a little. He was Jess Corbett, though, and he didn't get wishes or hopes or daydreams. Not now, not ever. Because whenever he touched anything, or even got close to touching it, it always turned out the same. *Bad.*

That was a thought that depleted him as he dropped his notes on a worktable, then marched out of the stable without so much as a goodbye. And it was a thought that still depleted him as he spun tires on the dirt road toward the lake, driving much too fast on what amounted to little more than a wide path that barely ever saw automobile traffic. It was also the thought that was still depleting him when he missed a turn in the road, spun off to the side trying to overcorrect in order to get back to where he needed to be, then plunged straight down into the ravine and finally, after a long, bumpy descent, came to a slow, jerky stop only when he hit a tree.

Missed opportunities...that was the only thing on his mind as Jess Corbett lost consciousness in one of the most out-of-the-way areas on the entire Corbett estate. Around him, the early evening shadows threatened to carry him along into the night, where the darkness would have no choice but to swallow him into oblivion or cradle him until morning.

CHAPTER FIVE

THE jingle of her cell phone awoke Julie with a start, and she immediately rolled over on her side to look at the clock on her bedside stand. It was a little after three. At this time of the night, the only phone call that could conceivably come in would be about a hospital emergency, so Julie was already sliding out of bed, preparing herself, mentally, for whatever was about to happen. "Hello," she said groggily, stifling a yawn after she'd clicked on.

"It's Rafe Corbett. Sorry to wake you up, Julie," he said. "Wasn't sure who else to call, so…"

He paused, and Julie responded without waiting for him to finish. "Not a problem. And I'm on my way, Rafe. Give me ten minutes to grab a shower and get dressed, then I'll be out the door. See you there in twenty, tops." Her feet dropped to the floor and she propelled herself up. "So, what's the emergency? Can you give me some idea of what should I be expecting when I get there?"

"It's not a hospital emergency," Rafe said. "It's personal. Jess..."

He hesitated, and she heard his audible sigh. Suddenly, the hair on her arms stood up.

"I haven't been able to get ahold of him. I've been trying for hours, and I wondered... Actually, Johnny told me the two of you spent some time together earlier today...that would be yesterday now, wouldn't it? Anyway, I was wondering if you knew where my brother was going after he left there? Did he say anything to you, or give you any kind of indication what he was going to do?"

She slid back down to the bed, sat on the edge of it, blinked hard a couple of times to clear her head, which wouldn't clear because an image of Jess planted itself in the forefront. "I'm sorry Rafe, but I don't know. He left in...well, we'd had a little disagreement, I suppose that's what you could call it, and he left."

"Was he angry?"

"Not really. More like he was quiet." And now she was blaming herself. Jess had been good, but she'd been…unresponsive. "I heard him drive off, but it was probably ten hours ago by now. Maybe even closer to eleven." Her stomach was beginning to churn. "I mean, I'm sure he's okay, Rafe. He probably just wants to be alone, or maybe he had an appointment to meet someone, or a hot date. So have you called the police department? Maybe Rick knows where he is."

"I've made the calls. No luck anywhere. And as far as I can figure out, you were the last person to see him. You're probably right, though, that he's okay. Hopefully on that hot date you mentioned, losing track of time. I mean, that would be good…my brother dating again."

An image she definitely didn't want in her mind.

"Or maybe he's off doing the solitary-man thing. We Corbett men have always liked our alone time. That's probably what this is about. Just Jess doing what he does."

Rafe's words sounded good on the surface, but nothing inside them sounded convincing to Julie. In fact, they sounded just the opposite, which caused the lump in her stomach to double instantly. "He's always been a little headstrong."

Putting it mildly. "So, you know what, Rafe? I could go out, have a look around." She wasn't sure where, but the rest of the night was shot for her. Too much worry and guilt equaled no more sleep for her until Jess was found. "Cruise up and down a few streets and see if I can spot his car. Check the all-night diner out on the highway, and Will Brassard's bar. I could also stop by the hospital and see if he's there, maybe in one of the on-call rooms. He was hanging around there earlier, just watching, so maybe he's gone back. Would it help if I went out?" Truthfully, it would be like looking for that proverbial needle in the haystack, but searching out that needle would be better than simply sitting around, waiting for it to appear.

"I don't really see much point to it, Julie. I actually think he might have gone back to the city. Jess is, well…unpredictable. Anyway, I appreciate the offer, and as soon as my brother checks in, I'll let you know. Thanks, and sorry to have bothered you."

The click of Rafe's phone was like the rumble of ominous thunder in her ear. Then, suddenly, she was alone in the dark, worrying about Jess.

"He's a loner, but he's not irresponsible," she reasoned with the emptiness around her. "He's abrupt, but not inconsiderate." In other words, she didn't believe he'd simply left Lilly Lake without a word to anybody. Especially *not* without saying something to his brother.

That was the belief that got her showered and dressed in record speed, and moved her out the door to her car. It was also the belief that put her behind the steering-wheel for the next hour and a half, driving up and down deathly quiet streets where the only signs of life were the moths that flickered around the incandescent glow given off by the streetlights, and all-night dives with their flickering neon welcomes.

"Maybe he's back at his cabin by now," Will Brassard suggested. Will was still hard at work in his own pub, cleaning up after the last customer had gone home. Julie liked Will. They'd been friends back in the day. Never close friends, but more than acquaintances.

Propped on a bar stool, drinking coffee left over from the sober-up pot Will always made for his last-of-the-night stragglers, Julie was glad for the warmth of the beverage. Even though the

April early morn wasn't so chilly now, something about being out all alone in the earliest hours was disquieting, maybe even a little sad. "I've called him every fifteen minutes for the last hour or so, and if he was anywhere near here, he'd have answered. I have an idea Rafe's been calling just as often as I have."

"Jess would answer...*if he could.*"

If he could... But what if he couldn't? *That* was the thought she didn't want to think. The one she could see reflected on Will's face. "Or maybe he's too far away now. Not in a good reception area. Could be, too, he simply forgot to turn on his phone."

"Or we might have to face the possibility that he's hurt," Will said, then tossed down his bar rag. "Look, there's no point standing around here wondering about it. Jess is a firefighter...one of *us...*" Meaning the unmistakable bond between all firefighters. "I'm going to call out a few volunteers and go have a look. As best as I can remember, there are probably four different ways to get back to his cabin, so by first light we should be able to get them all covered pretty quickly."

"Well, normally I'm not so reactionary, but that

may be a good idea. Jess is…" She really didn't have the right words to describe what she was trying to say. Sad. Impulsive. Lost. All accurate, but she didn't think they truly conveyed what Jess was going through right now. And to describe him in any more detail would give Will, or anybody listening in, cause to think she had feelings that went beyond simple friendship.

"He's Jess," Will supplied, then chuckled. "Isn't that what people always said about him? He's Jess."

Rafe was dependable. And Jess was Jess. "But Jess, being Jess, isn't irresponsible. Impulsive, yes. Stubborn, definitely. But not irresponsible. So, where do you want me to search?"

Will shook his head. "Can't let you do it, Julie. This could get dangerous, considering some of the territory we're going to have to cover."

"I know the area," she argued.

"But you haven't lived here for years. So you might have forgotten…"

"Can't stop me, Will." She sat down her coffee mug. "I'm a paramedic, remember? Worked in New York City. Seen tough, done tough, *am* tough. Considering the part of the city I worked in, a walk in the woods is a piece of cake. I'd rather do this with you and your men, but if you're not going to let me, then I'll be out there on my own."

"You haven't changed," he said, motioning her to the front door with him. "Stubborn when you were a kid, stubborn now." He chuckled. "In a lot of ways, just like Jess."

"Well, the *just like Jess* part I might have to debate with you. Actually, the part about not changing, too. Because I *have* changed. Back when I used to be stubborn, I didn't have anything to back it up but a bad attitude and some pretty ill-conceived ideas. Now I have skills you'll need out there if Jess is injured." She prayed, though, they wouldn't be needed.

Jess expelled an irritated sigh. He wasn't hurt so much as trapped. And at some point, when someone noticed him missing and came to find him, that whole embarrassment thing was going to kick in. But on the bright side, he wasn't hanging upside down. That was the only point of consolation he'd had over these past, interminably long, boring hours. He'd worked a couple of rescues where the victim trapped inside the car had been hanging upside down, or in some other uncomfortable position. So sitting here in his seat, with his damned foot trapped under the gas pedal so tight he couldn't move it without causing at least two or three significant metatarsal fractures, with a couple of broken phalanges thrown in there for good measure, while it wasn't comfortable, it certainly wasn't as uncomfortable as it could have been. The thing that probably hurt the most was the abrasion on his cheek that had happened as a result of the air bag inflating. That, and a splitting headache.

"Okay, now would be a good time to come and get me," he said to his cell phone, which wasn't picking up any kind of a signal. Not that he thought anybody would come for him. At least, not now. Not in the middle of the night. Actually, according to his watch, going on to morning. Of course, the big thing was, with the way he kept himself isolated, how long would it be before anybody actually started to miss him? Well, the answer to that was ten hours now, and counting.

"Ten hours," he muttered, shutting his eyes.

Ten empty hours where he'd done everything in his power not to think about anything. Problem was, the one thing...the one *person*...he couldn't keep out was Julie. In fact, even now, in the dark, sitting at the bottom of a ravine, he could still see her as clearly as if she were here.

"No way he'd take his car up that road!" Will exclaimed. He was pacing back and forth at the entrance to a very rough service road leading to the far side of the lake. "I mean, I was down that way a couple months ago, on a routine inspection, and it's bad."

"But it's a shortcut to the lake," Julie argued. And the place she and Jess had made love for the first time.

"If you're crazy enough to take it."

"And Jess is Jess," she reminded him, visoring her eyes and looking down the road as far as she could see in the emerging light. "Nobody's seen him anywhere else, so this is the last place to try, if we think he stayed on the estate." Intuition told her he had. Or maybe that was her heart indulging in some wishful thinking.

"Then we're going in on foot, because I can't

risk getting our department vehicles banged up if we don't know for sure he's down there."

"How about horseback?" Rafe called down from his mount, Donder. He was riding with Johnny and Rick. With them, they had brought another horse, a fine-looking bay filly Molly had named Lollipop. Lollipop was saddled, but without a rider. "The four of us will go in, take the road all the way down to the turn, then let you know what we find."

"Works for me," Will said. "And in the meantime, I'm going to send a couple of people back around to the other side to make sure we didn't miss anything. Also, I've got someone out on the road to Jasper, which is the way he'd have to go if he was returning to the city. Oh, and Rafe, I did call his department, talked to his chief, let him know we were looking for Jess, in case he turns up back in the city. And, um…well, now's not the time to talk about this, but they're concerned about him."

Julie shut her eyes, rubbed her forehead. Maybe she should have said something to Rafe about Jess's proclivity for taking risks, but invading Jess's privacy…it just didn't sit well with her. Jess might be a little out there, as far as some of his coworkers were concerned, but that didn't mean he was crazy, or a danger to himself or anybody else, for that matter. He was simply a man who was trying to work out his issues his own way, and she respected that. Sure, it worried her. But, deep down, she trusted Jess to do the right thing because that, too, was part of being Jess. "He just took in a little smoke," she said, trying to head off the conversation. "I was the paramedic who treated him that night, and it wasn't anything serious." Okay, so she wasn't being exactly forthcoming with everything but, somehow, she felt the need to protect Jess. Especially now, when he wasn't there to defend himself. "And right now we really do need to keep looking for him."

Will opened his mouth to speak, had second thoughts, then simply nodded. "She's right. Let's get back to work."

"So, is the bay for me?" Julie asked.

Rafe nodded. "You ride as well as the rest of us. And once we get to the bend, we're going to split up in pairs. So…" He pointed to the horse, and Julie mounted without hesitation.

"Do you know what Will's talking about?" Rafe whispered to her, as they headed out.

"What I know is that your brother has received more commendations in the short time he's been in the department than most people receive in the course of a career. The rest of it he'll have to tell you about. He's a good firefighter, Rafe. He cares."

"You're a loyal friend, Julie. Too bad he didn't hang on to you years ago. Things might have turned out differently for him."

Things might have turned out differently for her, too. But there really was no point in going over all the *what ifs,* because they didn't matter, and sometimes all they did was cause heartache.

"I see his car!"

Jess's eyes shot open and he looked at his watch. Eight o'clock. He'd been here, what? Fourteen, fifteen hours now? The effects of mild dehydration were beginning to set in, and his muscles were cramping something fierce. Plus, he was downright hungry and his throat was sore, partly from the dehydration, partly from giving in to frustration several times and simply yelling for help.

"Down at the bottom of the ravine. Up against a tree!"

Jess tapped the horn to let them know he was fine, but it didn't sound, the way it hadn't sounded every other time he'd tapped it in the past dozen or so hours. So he shouted, to no avail, unless the chipmunks scampering around the base of the pine tree just outside the car cared to listen.

"Any sign of life?"

"Not yet. I'm going down."

Was that Rick Navarro's voice? Rick and… Johnny Redmond, he thought.

"No, I'm going down," another voice shouted, and it didn't take any guessing to know who that was. It was Julie. She was taking charge.

Jess heaved a heavy sigh of relief, and relaxed.

"You don't do rescues, Rick," she continued.

"Go, Julie," Jess whispered. "Show them what you're made of." Good stuff. No, great stuff. In spite of himself, he enjoyed watching her rise to the occasion. The thing was, there was always this niggling thought just on the edge of his mind reminding him that she could have been his. She'd loved him back then, told him all the right things, wanted all the things that would have made for a great life. Sure, they had been young. And that had been part of his excuse for running out on her. The other part... Damn, why did his mind do this to him? Why did he have to keep replaying the way he'd messed up, first with Julie, then with Donna? With his whole damned life? "Shut up," he whispered to himself. "Shut the hell up!" Like that would stop the barrage of thoughts.

"But I do have that experience," Julie went on. "I'm trained. So I'll go down there first. And, Rafe, tell Will to get emergency equipment in here right now! Don't know what I'm going to find, but I want to be prepared. Also, I want an ambulance ready and waiting, and alert the E.R. that we'll be bringing Jess in shortly."

"Won't need an ambulance," Jess whispered. But then he began to worry. Julie, Rafe... It was his fault they were here. His fault they were putting themselves at risk to rescue him. Part of him wished everybody would go away and just let him work out his demons right then and there... Get it right in his head first, even if it took another day or two. Then come and rescue him. With Julie in charge, though, that wasn't going to happen. Truth was, he liked the barrier of avoidance he'd raised around himself. Once he learned how to keep it up all the time he'd be fine. *Just fine...* he thought, staring out the windshield, listening to the voices up above him.

"Rafe, Rick...once I'm down," Julie called, "one of you be prepared to follow me after you know what I need, and one of you stay up top."

"Damn it," Jess muttered. "How many more ways can I mess up my life?"

Lucky for him, he didn't have time to count the ways, as Julie's voice rang out from somewhere in front of the car just in time to save him from an even deeper descent into his own private hell of regrets. "Jess, can you hear me?"

"Yes," he shouted at the top of his lungs, which wasn't very loud.

"Jess, answer me!"

She was getting closer.

"Jess?"

"I'd answer if I could," he said, his voice traveling only into the windshield then stopping. Then he dropped his head back against the headrest and waited. What else could he do?

No answer. She could see the car ahead. It had cleared several large rocks, any number of trees and thankfully was sitting on all four tires, looking like it had taken a cruise down the hill and decided to come to a rest against the pine tree. Car was a mess, and she was praying Jess wasn't. But he wasn't answering, which worried her. So she doubled her pace, until she was practically running.

"Jess, answer me! Jess!" She was almost there. Couldn't see anything in the rear window from her vantage point. Nothing moving. Nothing obviously bloodied and mangled, though, thank God.

"Anything yet?" Rafe called from up top.

"Car's totaled. Can't see anybody inside." And most of her didn't want to take a look. But she was closing in, moving even faster… "Jess, can you hear me?"

No answer, but…was that something moving in there? A hand…waving? "Got a visual on something," she yelled, sprinting around the side of the car and coming to a stop on the driver's side. Sucking in a deep breath, she braced herself to look in, and saw…Jess, and he was grinning at her. Sitting there, grinning the grin of one mighty embarrassed man. Immediately, the tension drained from her, and she said a silent prayer of thanks. Then yanked open the car door so hard it hurt her shoulder. "What the hell are you doing?" she yelled at him, immediately dropping to her knees, pulling out a penlight and flashing it in his eyes.

"Waiting for you to come find me," he whispered. "Nice bedside manner, by the way."

"Probably better than you deserve. You had us scared to death, Jess. Half of Lilly Lake is out looking for you, your family…well, they can tell you how they've felt for the last several hours. And here you are, grinning." Eyes reactive. Bright, actually. "Got him," she yelled. "Alive, apparently well enough."

"Definitely well enough," he said. "No internal injuries, nothing serious, unless you consider humiliation an injury."

She gave him a fleeting glance, then mustered up a grin of her own. A very mocking grin.

"Well, you know what they say about your worst humiliation being someone else's momentary entertainment."

"What? No sympathy for the wounded man?" he teased.

Letting down, now that the emotional edge was off the moment, Julie gave herself over to a laugh—more of relief than anything else. "You're incorrigible, Jess. Do you know that? Has anybody ever told you how incorrigible you are?"

"Not quite so nicely as you put it. But in other words...yes. I've heard that a time or two in my life. Oh, and thanks. I'm glad it's you who came down to witness one of my less glorious moments."

"Less glorious moment...I'm glad that's all it was, Jess."

"You were scared, too?"

She nodded. "Back when I was a paramedic, the discovery was the part I didn't like. That moment when you don't know if your patient is alive or dead, that instant when you open the car door to find out... I loved that part where I got to take care of them, but I hated the discovery."

"I'm sorry you had to go through that with me,"

he said gently, reaching out to brush a thumb across her cheek.

One touch, and her heart raced. That's all it took from Jess. Then, now…that's all it had ever taken. To fumble her way around the realization that she still had strong feelings, Julie diverted her attention by taking Jess's blood pressure. Put everything she had into the simple task, gave it her undivided attention. Or, at least, tried. But even strapping the blood-pressure cuff to his upper arm caused… Oh, no! Those familiar twinges! She focused even harder on her task, squeezed her eyes shut as hard as she could to listen…to block him out totally.

Then, when she was done, and there was no way to avoid looking at him again, Julie pulled the stethoscope from her ears, braced herself to be professional and looked point blank at Jess. "Seriously, what happened to you? How did you end up here? If it's my fault, I'm sorry. I didn't mean to be so…"

"What I did was missed the turn. Haven't been down this road for years and I underestimated it. Meaning I took a detour straight down the embankment and hit the tree. And it's not your fault,

Julie. We're not making it click right between us yet, and that's all it was. It didn't result in…this." He pointed down to the way his foot was wedged underneath the gas pedal. "Would have climbed out, but I'm on the verge of snapping a few vital parts of my foot. Maybe have a wrenched knee and shoulder, too. Decided to sit this one out and wait for someone to come find me."

"*You* sitting around, waiting it out? What's this world coming to?" She bent down, took a look. Not only was his foot wedged under the pedal, it was actually locked into something underneath the dashboard. "It's pretty stuck, Jess."

"That's your professional opinion?" He relaxed back into the seat, but didn't take his eyes off Julie. "So, what's the verdict?"

"Describe your sensation to me."

"Other than being mighty glad to see you?"

"Am I going to have to call your big brother down here in order to get a straight answer out of you?"

"Okay, you win. I'll be more serious. I don't think my foot is broken. I can wiggle my toes, twist my ankle a fraction of an inch. No excruciating pain. Circulation's still pretty good, I think."

All of it good. Had he not been taking in every tiny move she made, she'd have sighed a sigh of relief over that one, but she didn't want to give herself away. Not even in the little things. Definitely didn't want Jess to think she cared in any way more than superficially. "Need help extricating him," she yelled back up. "And, Rafe, I may have some orthopedic injuries, so you should come down here and have a look. Oh, and a definite yes on the ambulance, because we're going to have to take him out on a stretcher." She glared over at Jess. "No arguments."

"Don't need a stretcher," Jess argued anyway.

Julie smiled at him. "This is the second time you've been my patient, and the second time you *have* to do what I tell you. So you might as well loosen up and go with it, because you don't have another choice." Then she reached over and squeezed his hand. "I'm glad you're injured and not gone."

"Injured and not gone?"

"Well, slightly injured. And, yes. Injured and not gone."

"What you're telling me is that people thought I'd up and left Lilly Lake without telling anybody?" he asked, sounding regretful. "I guess I deserve that, don't I, with the way I act sometimes?" He shrugged. "I think I have some apologies to make, especially to my family."

Julie uncapped a bottle of water she pulled from her emergency pack and handed it to him. "Look, I understand. What you went through losing your fiancée was…well, I can't even begin to imagine. And I'm sure it catches up with you. You're right, though, that there was some thinking along the line of you just leaving without saying anything to anybody. People do expect that from you, Jess. That's how you've always been. But I knew you wouldn't do it right now, not when Rafe needs you to help him with the hospital plans, especially with Edie getting ready to deliver. I mean, you've got a whole, long list of faults, and I'll be glad to go over them with you, in detail, once we get you out of here…" She smiled at him. "But you're not inconsiderate."

"Look, I know we've had our differences in the past… I said things, did things that were really stupid. So I do appreciate your sympathy toward me now, even though I don't deserve it." He drank greedily from the bottle, then heaved a sigh of relief. "Now, let me guess. You were the one who initiated the search."

"Something like that. Rafe called and—"

"I'm pretty sure *he* was one of those who came down on the side of me going back to the city without telling anybody. I think, over the years, Rafe has borne the brunt of my lifestyle more than anyone else. Borne it, compensated for it, tried explaining it away to other people. So he'd be the first one who'd expect me to bolt." He shrugged. "And I can't blame him."

"He was worried, Jess. Really worried, so don't fault him for anything because there's not much anybody can do in the middle of the night. He and Johnny saddled up at first light, though, along with Rick, and they rode. I went to see Will, who got some volunteers together, and… well, this is where we are. Oh, and just so you'll be prepared, Will did call your department in New York City and talked to your chief."

"And Steve said…"

"Don't know for sure *what* he said, but I think

it was probably what you'd expect him to say. You do go against the grain, you know."

"Which means Rafe knows everything. Meaning he expects even less of me now than he did before."

"So you should probably be the one to tell your brother what's going on with you so he won't think any less of you. I checked on you, Jess. After your smoke inhalation, I was worried because of some of the rumors I'd heard. So I checked, and I found out…"

"That they don't like the way I work. That I take risks…big risks."

"It's not so much the *way* you work. You've done amazing things in a short amount of time. But the risks you take…" She nodded. "That's the thing, I think. Those risks…"

"Save lives," he snapped. "Which is what my job is about. See, Julie, you don't like that first discovery, and I understand that. But that's where I shine. It's what I do best. It's why I'm a firefighter and not a doctor."

"It's also why you've had so many commendations. *And reprimands.* And, no, I haven't mentioned this to Rafe or anybody else because, as dumb as this may sound, considering that I worked so closely with the fire department and respected the rules, I think what you've done is admirable. I also think that you know exactly what you're doing each and every time you rush in. But to always put yourself in the way of harm, to put yourself out there in front of everybody else…"

"It's not always black and white out in the field, Julie. You, better than most, should understand that."

"I do. I've been out in that very same field. But the rules aren't made to be broken."

"Sometimes, though, they can't be followed."

Julie heaved a frustrated sigh. What he said was true. She couldn't argue the point. Especially not when Jess had been personally responsible for saving dozens of lives that might have otherwise been lost. He *did* know what he was doing. He *did* shine at the discovery. It was a salvation for many, and the cause of fearful dread for some. "Look, I'm not going to talk about this right now because the men are on their way down the hill and we need to figure out how to get you out of this mess. But later, Jess. We're going to talk about it later and, in the meantime, you might want to say something to Rafe because he's going to find out. Be fair to him, okay? Let him hear it from you."

"Thank you," he said, lifting the water bottle to his lips again.

"What for? I haven't done anything yet."

"You've done more than you know," he said. "Much more than you know."

CHAPTER SIX

BASICALLY, there was nothing wrong. According to the chart, Jess was bruised, with an air-bag abrasion to his right cheek, he did have a marginally sore shoulder of no consequence, slight concussion with no aftereffects, his knee was a little puffy but none the worse for wear and his foot was, according to Rafe, *just a little bit sprained.* Julie was glad to read the results of a couple of hours of tests. Now he could go home. "I'm on my way to give him the good news now," she said to Rick Navarro in passing.

"Well, say something to him about his driving, too, while you're at it," Rick quipped.

Suddenly, she prickled with defensiveness. "It wasn't like he intentionally drove off the road. Accidents happen. We see the results here in the E.R. all the time."

Rick arched skeptical eyebrows, then shrugged.

"Whatever," he said indifferently. Which made Julie prickle all the more.

"Do you think he did it on purpose? Is that what this is about?"

"What I think, Julie, is that Jess lives large and maybe not too cautiously. That's all I'm saying. Anything you want to infer from that, well… infer away. Your guess is as good as mine when it comes to Jess Corbett."

Trouble was, with her, it wasn't a guess. She knew. "It was an accident," she said emphatically. "He missed the turn."

"He missed the turn in an area *no one* travels. Think about it, Julie. Before you go getting yourself involved with Jess, just think about it. Okay?"

"I'm not getting involved with him," she said, trying hard to keep all inflection from her voice. "We dated years ago. And now…we're friends in the loosest sense of the word."

"Friends in the loosest sense of the word don't take offense the way you just did. And they don't go all red in the face either." He sucked in a sharp breath, let it out slowly. "Look, Julie. I'm not exactly the best one to be giving relationship advice here. I mean, look at me, look at the mess my personal life's been in for a while. I made mistakes, bad mistakes. So I know how it feels to have mixed emotions the way you do with Jess. But just be careful where Jess is concerned. I know he's not the guy we grew up with, but sometimes he seems angry like he did back then, and I'm not talking about the surface kind of anger where you go blow off steam somewhere and it's over. Jess's emotion is pervasive. It's eaten its way into a deep place, and at some point, if you do get more involved with him, it's going to pull you in, too. So as a friend just watch out for yourself. Okay?"

Julie stepped across the hall and gave Rick a quick hug. "I appreciate your concern, Navarro. But it's not the way you think it is between Jess and me."

"Are you sure? Because I remember how you were with him the first time, remember that look you used to get on your face every time you saw him or someone talked about him. Saw it then, see it now. Go look in the mirror, Julie, if you don't believe me." With that, he headed down the corridor leading to Admittance while Julie turned and went down the corridor toward the cubicle where Jess was waiting, impatiently, to be dismissed.

"What I'm saying, Jess, is that you can't keep doing it." Rafe's voice lowered so not to be heard. "I appreciate you telling me, but it's not like I haven't been seeing this in you for a while."

"There's nothing to see. I do my job. People perceive me to be reckless, but I'm not. It's all a matter of interpretation."

"Is it? Because you're sitting out there at the cabin for two weeks, and I don't believe that it's because you needed a vacation or you inhaled a little smoke. You don't have to say the words, Jess. I know."

"Know what?" Jess snapped.

Out in the corridor, Julie stepped back, caught up in the dilemma about whether to let the brothers argue it out without her standing there, listening or breaking it up by barging in. Honestly, she thought the air needed to be cleared between Jess and Rafe…for Jess's sake as well as Rafe's. So she stepped back again, but not entirely away because what she heard next glued her to the spot.

Rafe looked his brother straight in the eye, determined to get through to him. "What the old man did to you. While he was beating the hell out of me, he was turning the psychological battle on you. Don't you think I heard the things he used to call you?"

"Just words," Jess said.

"Words," Rafe snorted. "Believe me, Jess, there were times when I was grateful he was only beating me. A bruise heals, but being told you're worthless doesn't."

Julie drew in a sharp breath. She'd known. Yet she hadn't known...not the extent of the abuse. And suddenly she could see Jess and Rafe as boys...Rafe with the bruises, Jess with the attitude and the strange, haunted look in his eyes. Too many people had known, too many people had found it easier to look away.

"I don't want to talk about it," Jess snapped. "He's dead. I've moved on."

"But to where, Jess?" Rafe asked. "You went to medical school, you joined the military, now you're a firefighter. Is that how you're going to live your life, always moving on?"

"You know, you got lucky, Rafe. Edie, Molly, another one on the way...you're one lucky guy and I envy you what you've got. I almost had some of it, but then I blew it. Stepped right in front of myself and put an end to something that could have been good because I know that I'm not the settling-down kind. But at least I recognize that…recognized that before it was too late. Donna and I…we didn't make it to the end. I pushed her away for her own good. At least, in my opinion it was for her own good. Told her I couldn't go through with it, then an hour later she was…" His words broke off. He shut his eyes.

"My God, Jess! I didn't know."

His eyes snapped back open. Angry eyes. Eyes filled with rage. "Well, you should have. Because that's how I've always been. It's who I am."

"Or who you choose to be."

"What the hell do you know about me, Rafe? Other than that we share blood, what the hell do you really know?"

"That you're running from the same thing I am…turning out like the old man. We hated him, and we see his traits in us. We're doctors, Jess. We followed in his footsteps there, and even though that's where I know I'm supposed to be, don't you think it bothers the hell out of me some days when I let myself think about it?"

"Except I'm not a doctor."

"Sure you are. You can deny it all you want, but it's still there inside you. Maybe buried a little deeper than it used to be. But still there. So it's got to scare you sometimes when you think about it, like it does me. I understand the fear of being like the old man. And I understand pushing people away so you don't have to face yourself, because that's what I did when I first met Edie."

"Well, you didn't push hard enough, and it worked out for you. I'm glad. But I'm not getting that close to anybody again because it's not what I'm supposed to have, not who I'm supposed to be. So, yes, maybe my life is always going to be about moving on, and that may include taking some of the bigger risks since I don't have to think about a wife and children first, in case I get killed, or critically injured. But I don't have a death wish, big brother. I don't do stupid things and nobody—*nobody*—is going to tell me the risks I take aren't necessary, because they are. And so you'll know, the only reason I even said something to you about what's been going on with me is because if I hadn't, Julie would have. She got on me about it even before you guys came down that hill and pulled me out of the car."

"Then good for Julie," Rafe said to his brother.

"Look, I'm sorry I didn't say something sooner. The thing is, none of it matters. I'm not going to change. I thought I could, but I can't. Julie couldn't change me all those years ago. When I thought she was pregnant, when I knew she wasn't... She wanted to be pregnant, Rafe. Wanted that baby. At the end of the day, when I was trying to look for a practical solution, all I really wanted was to get as far away from my mess as I could get. I knew she was hurt when she found out she wasn't pregnant, knew that somehow she'd built some fantasies around it, but I was glad it turned out like it did, Rafe. Glad I didn't have to deal with her pregnancy, glad I didn't have to deal with her, glad to get away. Then when Donna and I were... Damn it, Rafe! I looked at home design catalogues with her, picked out color patterns, got involved in the decision about which duvet to buy. I wanted to do it, should have been able to. But when she started talking about that satiny, mauve duvet that would go so well with throw pillows, that's when I knew I couldn't go through with it and all I wanted to do was get away from it…from her.

"Donna deserved that domesticity, she deserved that husband who really cared about the details the way she did. And it wasn't me. The more plans she made, the more I was sweating it out. Literally getting sick to my stomach. But trying to be all she needed me to be. In the end…" He shrugged. "I should have been honest with her from the start. Told her who I really am. Then turned my back on her before we got to the place where she expected a duvet."

Outside the curtain, Julie bristled. He'd been glad to get away from her? *Glad?* She'd always thought it had been fear, never expected to hear it described as something that had made him glad. And that hurt. "Here!" she said, whooshing through the curtain and thrusting the discharge papers at him. "Sign them, then drop them off at the desk on your way out the door!" She brushed past Rafe and started to exit, but Rafe caught her by the arm and held her in place.

"I didn't have time to thank you for rescuing my brother."

"It's my job. What I do. That's all it was," she said, fighting for control even though right now it wasn't coming through for her the way she wanted. Because right now all she wanted to do was get away from Jess, not have to look at him, not have to have these awkward, mixed emotions she was feeling give her away to the man who most didn't want to see them.

"Julie..." Jess said, shoving to the edge of the bed. "You heard what I just said to Rafe, didn't you?"

"You're accusing me of eavesdropping?"

"There's no expectation of privacy here. I know that."

"I didn't want to interrupt."

"But you're part of this."

"No, I'm not. Because there's nothing to be part of, Jess."

Jess tried to stand, but came up wobbly on his foot. Which Julie used to her advantage, and backed away even more.

"You said you were glad to get away from me, Jess. I would have understood if you said it was fear. I would have understood if you'd said you were confused. But glad?"

"Not in the sense of being happy. More like…"
She shook her head. "No. We don't have to do
this, don't have to do anything. I work here, I may
run into you from time to time since, technically,
I suppose you are my boss. There's nothing else,
though. And that's something else you can be
glad about." Maybe Rick was right about what
he'd seen, but he wasn't going to see it again.

"Can we just talk about it? Let me try to explain
what happened?"

"You know what, Jess? You can talk all you
want. I'm not going to stop you. But I'm not
going to be here to listen to you either. Summer
Adair's coming on duty, and she'll make sure
you're processed out. Or you can stay here. It's
your hospital. Do what you want."

By the time she'd cleared the E.R. doors and
was on her way to the cafeteria for a cup of hot
tea, Julie's hands were shaking. Then, by the
time that cup of hot tea was in hand and she was
sitting alone in the farthest corner of the room,
her back to everyone, her face to the window,
her gut was knotted. Finally, by the time she'd
raised the cup to her lips, she was fighting back
tears she refused to spill. Nobody made her cry.

Nobody had for a long, long time and Jess wasn't going to be the one to do it. He didn't deserve that distinction. So she fought back her case of threatening weeps by focusing on her to-do list, and refused—*refused*—to let anything sidetrack her. She had bandages to order and a drug cabinet to restock. In Julie Clark's life right now, that's all there was.

"I know. It was stupid. I was stupid." Jess stood at the window overlooking Gracie stables. Julie was in there, and while he couldn't see her, he did take some comfort in knowing that he hadn't totally driven her away from everything she loved.

"She's just hurt," Edie Corbett said. "Give her time."

Jess turned to face his sister-in-law. Wonderful woman. Great mother. Rafe was a lucky man. "Time? That's not going to heal anything. I hurt her. Took a time in her life when she was so vulnerable… You know about the pregnancy scare, don't you?"

"Rafe told me."

"Anyway, I shot off my mouth, said I was

glad to get away from all that mess I'd made. But back then she'd wanted that baby, and she'd been so hurt when she'd discovered she wasn't pregnant. Then the other day, what I said..."

Edie laid a comforting hand on his arm. "I don't know what's going on between you and Julie, but if it's something that's meant to be... friendship, more than friendship, you'll work through this."

"I can't do more than friendship," he said.

"Don't sell yourself short, Jess. Rafe did, yet look where he is now?"

"He's where he's supposed to be, with the right person."

"And you can't find that for yourself?"

"Oh, I probably can find it. It's what I do with it after I find it that's the problem."

"Well, maybe when it finds you, instead of the other way around, it, or *she,* will fight hard enough to help you overcome the obstacles. It can be done, Jess. Just look at me..." She patted her belly. "I fought hard for one of the Corbett boys, and won."

Edie was close to her due date now, and she really did glow. For a moment he caught himself wondering what Julie might have looked like at this point in her pregnancy, if she'd been pregnant. But as fast as that bit of melancholia hit him, he shook it away. "Rafe won."

"And you can't?" she asked. "Just look out that window, Jess. Maybe all you'll get out of this is a good friend, but isn't a good friend worth the effort?"

"But I don't want anything out of this."

"Then why do you keep staring out the window at her?"

Truth was, he didn't know. Even now, he was watching Julie simply stand there and stroke the gray Arabian's muzzle. What an astonishing thing, seeing how she could gentle an animal so easily. She could do that with people, too. With him... Already had with him. "Look, I think I need to hobble on out there and see if she'll talk to me. I do owe her an apology."

"Don't be too hard on yourself, Jess. No matter what you've done, or said, I know Julie won't be." Edie handed him the cane that was to be his companion for the next couple of weeks. "And if she doesn't want to listen this time, maybe she will next time, or the time after that."

Limping past Edie on his way out the door, Jess stopped and brushed a tender kiss to her cheek. "You know, if my brother hadn't found you first..."

Edie laughed. "Yeah, yeah. That's what they all say. Oh, and Jess, invite Julie in for dinner later on. Don't know if she's actually ready to sit down at a table with you, but if she is, tell her it's chicken cordon bleu."

"Think she'd come if you put me in the next room and shut the door?" he asked, stepping out onto the porch.

"That's always an option."

Making his very slow path down the porch steps and off in the direction of the barn, Jess debated with himself if he really needed to be doing this. He'd already put Julie through hell, and he truly didn't want to make the situation any worse. But he had to talk to her, or try. Had to tell her he was a hothead who blew off steam without thinking first.

"Are you supposed to be walking around?" she asked him, purposely avoiding eye contact. In fact, her back was to him as she brushed Ghazi and she didn't so much as glance over her shoulder at Jess. "I thought Rafe told you to stay off your feet for a couple of days."

"Since when do I listen to anybody?" Jess asked. "Isn't that what I do best? Not listen?"

She didn't answer him. Didn't say a word.

"Look, Julie. What I said…what you heard. You're right. I did mean it. But not the way you think."

"There really aren't too many ways to interpret it."

"Okay, so I'll admit it. I wasn't ready for what might have happened if you'd been pregnant. I was glad you weren't, and that was purely selfish on my part. But what I had going on in my life back then…"

"I was your mess. I get it. And believe it or not, I even get why you ran away. I was a little girl dreaming grown-up dreams. But to hear that you were *glad* to get away from me… I don't suppose I expected that. Not from you."

"I was glad, though. But not for the reasons you think. See, I almost bought into your fantasy. It scared me. I'll admit that. Settling down at seventeen into some kind of domestic arrangement, with a baby, no less. I don't think there are many seventeen-year-old boys out there who want that, or who even think that could be the outcome when they get sexually active. I sure didn't. And the way my old man was screaming at me... But the thing is, part of me actually believed I could make a go of it. I didn't want you near him, though. He'd have done to you what he did to Rafe and me, and I was too young to protect you from it." He cringed, thinking back to that time. The horrible things that had happened, the fear of what his old man would do. *What his old man had done.* "It is what it is, Julie. I can't go back and change it and even if I could, I probably wouldn't because I didn't want you dragged down to where I was. That's all I meant when I said I was glad to get away. I was. It gave me a new chance at life, and it gave you one as well. And look what you've done since then."

She finally whirled around to face him. "I appreciate your honesty, but so far all you've done is evade things that need to be dealt with, then get angry when you're backed into a corner. That's not who you are, Jess. Maybe you don't know that anymore, but that's not who you are." She expected anger, expected him to push her away like he did everybody else, but what she saw when she allowed herself to look into his eyes was sadness. "I'm sorry for your past, Jess. Sorry about Donna, too. Everybody is. The thing is, if you let people in, you'll make it easier on yourself. People want to be there for you but you make that impossible." She tossed her brush into a tack box and took Ghazi by the reins, ready to lead him back into the stable. "When I first came here, to Gracie House, even to Gracie Foundation, I pushed people away harder than anybody I've ever seen since. But Grace pushed back. She was the first one. And she made me realize that all my pushing...it was just fear. Here I was, thinking I was being all brave and tough, and when I opened my eyes to it, what I found was a scared little girl who simply didn't want to be hurt anymore."

"And the little boy who didn't want to be hurt anymore either."

Julie nodded. "So, aren't we the pair?"

"Can the pair be friends?" he asked, following her to the stall, where she settled Ghazi in. "I know we keep trying, but is there a chance we can actually do it? Or have we gone too far past that point?"

They'd been lovers but, given her feelings for him now, could they be *only* friends, or would that hurt too much? It was a brutal question, but an honest one for which she had no answer. "That's an age-old question, isn't it?"

"You mean because we…?"

She nodded. "I mean, I don't ever remember us being friends. We had the other thing going on…"

"Because we were kids. Kids aren't always that smart when it comes to, well, that part of life. Act first, think later."

"Like we did. Only I don't think we ever got to the part where we were thinking about anything, did we?"

He leaned against the doorjamb, took the weight off his foot. "Trust me, I was thinking. In fact, the only thing I was thinking about all those weeks was you."

She laughed. "Yeah, typical boy thoughts. And we both know what those are."

"Okay, so I'll admit I did have those thoughts.

I mean, come on. You were a looker. So how could a boy *not* have those thoughts?"

"A looker?"

"I'm just being honest here. But I thought about you in other ways, too. I liked your intelligence, liked the way you faced the challenges. Liked the way I felt when I was with you."

"I didn't know that."

"Because I was a typical guy and whenever we got together, all *those* things flew right out of my mind. So, do you think we can come to some kind of an understanding?"

"Why are you pushing me, Jess?"

"Because I still like your intelligence, still like the way you face challenges. Still like the way I feel when I'm with you. And—" he grinned "—you're still a looker. What can I say? I'm a man, I like to look."

In spite of herself, she laughed. How could she not? Even with his rough ways, Jess was a charmer. Had been when he was a boy, was more so now. And she was just as susceptible to that charm now as she had been when she'd been a girl. "So what am I supposed to do with that, Jess? Tell me, because I don't know."

"It's easy. Just accept me for who I am. And don't worry so much."

"Not worry? Are you kidding me? Because look what you do. You've been a firefighter for just a little under two years, and you're already a legend. It's a risky legacy, though. Who you are causes people to worry. So, I can accept you the way you are because that's not going to change and I don't think it has to, but the worry comes with it. It's conditional. And one more thing, while we're on the topic of worry. Tell me why you were out on *that* particular road. There are all kinds of speculations swirling around, nobody really understands why. But I want to understand, because it was dangerous, Jess. What you did was so dangerous."

He braced himself with a stiff breath. "Okay, in the interests of friendship, the truth. And it's not very exciting. I used to go out there when I was a kid. Loved that area because I had the lake at my front and the foothill at my back, with trees everywhere else. I always felt...protected there. It was a long way from the house, and I knew my old man wouldn't come that far looking for me. Rafe had his haven up at Hideaway

Bluff and that's where the two of us went to-gether. But I had my place down at what I called Lake's Edge. It was perfect, nobody even knew I went there, except you, and I just wanted to go back to…think. That's all it was."

"I always loved that area, too," Julie admit-ted, her eyes softening as she thought of Lake's Edge. "After the first time you took me there, I used to go out there myself sometimes when I wanted to be alone."

"I was thinking about you and me there, on the picnic blanket under that big old oak tree… I think I just wanted to spend a little time in a place where my life never seemed complicated."

"It did seem simple then, didn't it, being young, and in love? Nothing else in the world mattered while we were there." Sighing, Julie shut her eyes. "I wanted us to build a house there. Nev-er mind the impractical aspects of exactly how that could happen. I wanted a house, a proper Victorian with a wrap-around porch. White picket fence. Flower garden. Innocence of youth, even though I don't remember ever being inno-cent. But it's nice in a fantasy, isn't it?"

"Well, I never got around to imagining a house

there. But I liked the solitude. The safety. And the memories. Which is why I was on that road. I wanted to go back there and pretend everything was the way I wanted it to be. I missed the turn because I wasn't concentrating on the road." A glint came to his eye. "Amazingly, the images of us there are still pretty vivid. But that's all it was, I swear."

A soft smile crossed her lips. "You're incorrigible, Jess, but I believe you."

He stood, winced, bore down harder on the cane. "So, friends...*finally?*"

"Friends don't let friends stand too long on an injured foot." Immediately, she stepped to his side, slid her arm around his waist and her shoulder under his arm. "You need to sit down."

"I know why my aunt loved you," he said, as they made their way over to a bench near the tack room.

Julie chuckled, helping him down. "I think love is a strong word for how Grace felt about me. Maybe she liked me..."

"*Loved you.* Because you were strong."

"I had to be strong, because I wasn't very smart about pretty much everything I was doing. So I needed something to compensate for my lack."

"You mean, not very smart about us?"

That's not what she'd meant because, no matter how badly it had turned out between them, she'd never had any real regrets about her brief love affair with Jess. And in her mind it had been a love affair. First lovers were never very smart, though, were they? "Let's just say that I wasn't smart about a lot of things. Eager, I'll admit. Because I wanted you probably in the same way most teenaged girls want their first love. Also, I always knew more than anybody else. Couldn't be taught, or told..."

"And your parents?"

"You mean my *third* set of parents? The ones who left me before Grace took me in? What's there to say? They were probably decent people, but I didn't give them much time before I was looking for my way out, doing the things I knew would facilitate that."

"Three sets of parents? I don't suppose I ever knew that about you." He shifted on the bench and stuck his foot out, then bent down to adjust the hard plastic ortho boot Rafe had forced on him.

"When Grace took me in, I was on the verge of being declared a casualty. The state wanted to put me in a juvenile detention facility, wanted to lock me up until I was an adult, basically. Anyway, Grace found me. Took me in, and she respected me, Jess. She kept my wild-child ways private because she had faith in me. At least, that's what she always said. And you know what? I believed her. She was the only person I ever truly believed." She sat down next to Jess. "Now, I'm going to take that boot off you and see if your foot is swelling, because I'm betting it is."

"Then what?" he asked.

"After I adjust the straps, you either sleep here with the horses tonight or I help you back up to the house."

"It's swelling," he said, even before she'd bent down to have a look. "But it's worth it."

"How?" she asked as she slid the ortho boot off him.

"Because of this."

"What?"

"This." With that, Jess reached his hand over and turned Julie's face toward him. "You can stop me. Or not."

"This isn't the oak tree, Jess."

"And we're not kids."

And she hadn't been with a man since Jess. But he didn't need to know that. Didn't need to know anything. Neither did she, except...how, exactly, had this happened? How had they gone from nothing to friends to what was about to come into being in mere minutes?

"I don't do this with risk takers," she said, in her first effort to put him off. Flimsy effort, though. "And you're hurt. Your foot is definitely swelling. You need to go prop it up."

"Which has nothing to do with anything."

He still had her face cupped in his hand... strong hand, nice. Not baby-soft like she remembered from him, but rough. Disturbingly, arousingly so. Every fiber in her body was urging her to close the distance, crush herself to him, wrap herself around him and kiss him until she was too weak to draw breath. But every fiber in her body was also screaming that this was Jess, and she knew how it had to turn out with him. "Jess, um…this isn't…"

"Isn't what, Julie?" His head dipped toward her. "Tell me," he whispered.

"We can't do this. It's not us, not who we are anymore," she finally managed to say. On so many levels, though, she wanted this…yet on so many levels it scared her. But she didn't have time to think, didn't have to do the usual Julie Clark thing and make a list of pros and cons. Grace had taught her to do that before embarking on any unsure venture and this was as unsure as it got. However, as the list was forming in her mind, specifically the one with all the reasons why she shouldn't be doing this, his lips brushed hers and, oh, they were soft, yet not tentative in the least. Not demanding at first, though, like she remembered from him before. In fact, his kiss started like a casual stroll, a walk in the park, exploring the pleasantries. Almost chaste, but not quite. Perhaps like he was exploring his own boundaries.

His touch was skilled as he slid his hand up her back, as he traced the outline of her lips with the tip of his tongue. Jess had, indeed, moved on in his lovemaking, while she had chosen to stay behind, stay in the past. It was obvious in his every move, as it was surely as obvious to him in her every move.

"Jess," she murmured against his lips, with every intention of pulling back. But she didn't, as once she did it would be over. It would have to be over. So she answered the quest of his tongue by nibbling and sucking his bottom lip, eliciting a groan from him. And at the sound of his deep, guttural arousal, fire darted through her veins, coursed through her pores, made her burn and tremble in places where only Jess had caused that to happen before. And, as hard as she was trying to hold on to her reserve, to not show any outward excitation, she must have responded where Jess could feel it, because instantly his tongue flicked to part her lips and delve inside.

There was nothing left in her to fight against what she wanted. Nothing left of her list, nothing left of common sense, and this did defy every ounce of common sense she possessed. Accordingly, she indulged herself in that blissfully sensual, erotic experience, giving herself over to her own explorations.

This isn't good, she thought to herself, or maybe she murmured it aloud…she didn't know, didn't care as she scooted to press herself even closer to him, not even thinking about how they were sitting on the tack-room bench where anybody could see them. None of that mattered just then, because Jess kissed her the way she wanted to be kissed by him, the way she'd allowed no one else to do to her. Skillful, passionate, emotional… Her heavy sigh was testament to that, a testament to feelings she'd kept buried, and that, tomorrow, she would wish had stayed buried. Because for Julie it had to be everything, or nothing. That's just the way she was, the way Grace had taught her to be. But Jess didn't want that. She'd heard him say it… *I'm not getting that close to anybody again because it's not what I'm supposed to have, not who I'm supposed to be. So, yes, maybe my life is always going to be about moving on…*

The only thing he wanted was to move on emotionally. And emotionally all she wanted was to stay. That's all she'd ever wanted…that place where someone truly wanted her. Where that someone would never, ever leave her.

"Where are you, Julie?"

"What?"

"Where are you? Where did you go?"

It was only then that she realized she'd been the one to end the kiss, to pull back. To disengage herself completely from Jess. "What are we doing, Jess? We can't relive the past. Can't go back and make things right. So, what is this?" The uncertainty in her voice gave her away as she pushed herself away from him, bent down and fumbled to get the ortho boot back on him.

"I don't know, Julie. Wish I did, but I don't."

And he didn't want to figure it out. That was as plain on his face as embarrassment was on hers. "Okay, we've kissed. No big deal. Now I've got to get back to work."

"I never get it right with you, do I?" he said, taking hold of his cane and pushing himself off the bench. "Never have…"

Never will. He didn't say the words aloud, but she felt them in her heart. And they stung because what she didn't want to know had just become painfully obvious to her. She still had feelings for Jess Corbett. And he'd never stopped running away.

CHAPTER SEVEN

SHE was stunning, sitting astride Ghazi, bareback. He'd been watching her gentle the horse for two days now. Hadn't said a word to her, hadn't even gone close. His excuse was that he didn't want to spook the horse and everything seemed to spook that horse, except Julie. In truth, though, he didn't want to spook Julie.

Damn, he shouldn't have kissed her. Should have left well enough alone, especially since they'd come to an understanding. But the urge… well, he'd hoped it would be quelled. It wasn't, though. Didn't even come close to it. In fact, one kiss had whetted his appetite. He wanted more. But he knew the result of that, didn't he? Which made the acid churn bitterly in his stomach. One more screwup to add to his collection.

"She's making progress," Rafe said, sitting down next to Jess on the front porch. "Johnny wasn't sure that one was going to turn out good.

Too abused. But Julie has her way with horses, doesn't she? Probably one of the best horsewomen I've ever seen."

In answer, Jess shifted positions on the swing, then shifted his gaze to focus on a little chickadee hopping its way through the grass. Watching Julie, thinking about Julie…it was turning into a habit he had to break. Clearing his throat, he forced another thought into his head. "I looked over her plans for the emergency department, added some ideas of my own. They're good, within the existing structure. But I've been wondering if it's time to go beyond that structure and do something worthwhile for the whole area, considering that we've got the space, as well as the resources."

"Didn't think you wanted to get that involved in the hospital again."

"I don't…didn't. But right now there's nothing else to do. Can't go back to work. Can't even walk around without injuring myself. And if I spend another day staring at the walls—" *or Julie* "—I'll go crazy. So I might as well do something useful." Something *with* Julie.

Rafe chuckled. "So, as a last resort, you're

going to play at being a hospital owner? Which is fine with me, actually, because I could use some help."

"Well, don't go thinking I'll be returning to medical practice, because I won't. But I want to take a stab at seeing how we can manage more for Lilly Lake. There's a need. A big need. And before you tell me that's what you've been trying to get me to do for months, I know that. I should have listened to you. But I didn't, and I can't change it."

"Better late than never. And so you'll know, I'm not going to kick you in the butt over it, since I didn't exactly want to take up the cause either."

"But you got lucky and ended up with a good life here," Jess said, almost on a wistful sigh. "How is Edie doing this morning? She seemed a little tired at breakfast."

"I think she's anxious to get this pregnancy over with. I mean, I can't even begin to imagine what she's going through, but for me this is turning into the longest nine months of my life. Last summer when Edie and I met seems like an eternity ago in some ways, and a moment ago in others. And this pregnancy…" He drew in the deep breath of a contented man. "It's good, Jess. Endlessly long, nothing I'd ever thought I'd be dealing with, but good. A year ago if anyone had told me that in the very near future I'd be a dad, *twice*..." He grinned. "It changes everything."

"And who would have ever thought that you'd actually end up settling here in Lilly Lake? Edie has done nice things for you, big brother. Real nice things, and you deserve the good life with her."

"Any chance that you and Julie...?"

Jess shook his head before Rafe had finished the question. "With Julie, I find more ways to screw up than most people could even think of. And not just little things."

"For what it's worth, I think you'd be good together."

"It's not worth anything. Julie and I have bad history. You know that. And I'm not doing anything to make it better. In fact, I think I made it worse." He chanced a glance at Julie, who had brought Ghazi around to the near side of the paddock. She was still on the Arabian's back, but she was leaning forward, almost lying across the horse's neck, stroking his muzzle and, if he knew

Julie, probably whispering sweet nothings in his ear.

"How?"

"Kissing her."

Rafe grinned. "That's all? You're worried about a kiss? Usually, that's the start of something."

"After she heard me say I was glad to get away from her?"

"Well, there is that. So, did she slap you?"

Jess shook his head. "As a matter of fact, she was pretty blasé about the whole thing. Didn't seem to care one way or another."

"But you do?" Rafe arched skeptical eyebrows, staring at his brother. "Because aren't you the one who keeps telling me he doesn't want a commitment?"

"A kiss isn't a commitment."

"Could be the prelude to a commitment, though."

"It wouldn't work, couldn't work."

"I recall saying pretty much the same thing myself. Now I'll be the first to admit I was wrong."

"But we're not alike, Rafe. Never have been. You were the one who stood up to the old man and got hit for it, while I was the one who kept quiet and flew under his radar a lot of the time."

Rafe shook that off with a shrug. "Wasn't in your nature to fight back. Sure as hell was in mine, though. But it doesn't matter now, does it?"

"Well, maybe not as far as I'd hoped." Jess glanced out again at Julie. It was hard to keep his eyes off her, hard not thinking about her. "Did you know that only time he ever beat me was when he thought Julie was pregnant? He overheard Julie and me talking about it. Said bad things about Julie after that. Came after me with a shovel."

"Son of a…" Rafe snapped. "If you'd told me…"

"What would you have done? Come home, beat him. Or let him beat you again? You were already out of it, Rafe. I didn't want you coming back into it."

"But you didn't go to Aunt Grace, did you?"

Jess shook his head. "The old man was crazier than I'd ever seen him. I didn't want Aunt Grace, or Julie, involved because I was afraid he might hurt them, too."

"It always dumbfounded me how he could be

such a good doctor, and such a miserable excuse for a human being."

"Some things can't be explained. Once I asked Aunt Grace why he was like he was and she told me it didn't matter. That there were some questions in life that didn't have answers."

Rafe nodded. "The old man was one of those questions, I guess."

"I guess," Jess said. "Anyway, he'd made some threats against Julie, said he'd have her sent away. Remember Judge Frayne? He used to play golf with the old man. Anyway, he said he'd go to the judge and see to it that Julie was removed from Aunt Grace's custody and sent to a juvenile home. He accused Julie of getting pregnant only so she could get her hands on Corbett money, and I think that was the first time I ever stood up to him, told him to leave her alone or I'd be the one taking the shovel to him"

"Bet that didn't go over well."

"He tried hitting me again."

"And...?"

"I got him first. He was old, drunk. I was young, angry. He came at me, and..." Jess shrugged. "That's when I knew I had to get away. I wanted to kill him, Rafe. All that anger in me, I was afraid I would."

"This was all before she'd discovered she *wasn't* pregnant?" Rafe asked.

"The sequence is all kind of a blur." He would never tell anybody, not even Rafe, that Julie already knew she wasn't pregnant, but had kept it a secret. She wasn't being deceitful or manipulative, even if that's what he'd accused her of. But that's how it would have seemed if he'd said she'd known for days and hadn't told him. "But I'm pretty sure I didn't know she wasn't pregnant at that time."

"So, what happened after that?"

The part of the story he'd never told. The part that was still so painful. But this was Rafe. It was time he knew. "First let me say I was confused. I loved Julie, but I had to get away, had to physically put myself in another place. I was scared that I would kill the old man, that it would go beyond threats or feelings."

Rafe swallowed hard. Didn't say a word. Just put his arm around his brother's shoulders for support. "There were too many things for me to deal with. I didn't know what to do, couldn't think, couldn't function. So I went down to the stables one day, decided to take Storm out for a ride, just to get away for a while and clear my head. But the old man was standing there in the middle of the aisle, proud as punch, with a gun in his hand." He swallowed hard. "Standing next to Storm's body. He told me the horse wasn't mine, that nothing in this world was mine, that he could give and take anything from me he wanted to… my horse, my aunt, my pregnant girlfriend."

"I'm sorry, Jess. I never knew what happened to Storm. I figured the old man did something to him, but I didn't want to ask, probably because I didn't want to know how far he'd go."

"Like I said, I wanted to kill him, Rafe. I swear to God, I really wanted to kill him that day. And that shovel he'd taken to me…I took it to him. Knocked him to the ground with it, then stood over him. Had my foot on his chest, shovel ready to swing. And he looked up at me and laughed. Told me I didn't have the guts to go through with it. But for a moment, he was wrong. I did, because he'd killed my horse, and threatened my aunt, as well as the girl I loved. The girl I thought was carrying my baby. The only thing that stopped me from going through with it, though, was that he *was* right. I *didn't* have it in me. Didn't want to have it in me. It was actually the day I decided I wanted to help, not hurt."

"I'm sorry you had to go through it. Sorry you didn't let me help you"

"Help me get through what? Being just like the old man? Because that's who I turned into for a little while, Rafe. The old man. When I found out Julie wasn't pregnant, I accused her of trying to trap me. Said the same things to her the old man had said to me. Heard these ugly, hurtful words coming out of my mouth, and I couldn't stop them. That's who I was, who I'd turned myself into."

"I'm not going to let you sit here and criticize yourself, Jess. We both lived in the same hell. It was the old man who did this. Not us. Not me. Not you. He's the one who put you in that place, who made his demands, who killed Storm."

"And I'm the one who killed…well, so many dreams. Donna's, Julie's… But to Julie's credit, she's been good to me since she came back to Lilly Lake. Much better than she should be, considering what I put her through. Better than I deserve from her."

"And after that you two never connected at all over the years?"

Jess shook his head. "I thought about it, but I didn't know how. I did ask Aunt Grace about her several times, and all she would ever tell me was that Julie had a good life going, that she was doing well for herself, that she was happy. So why would I want to interfere in that?"

"Did Aunt Grace ever know what happened? About the pregnancy scare, or what the old man did?"

"If she did, she never said anything to me. But she wouldn't have, would she? Aunt Grace took care of things quietly and she may have had something to do with how I never heard from the old man again after I left Lilly Lake. Not one, single word." Jess sighed. "Anyway, I appreciate the hospitality. It's been nice staying here with you, Edie and Molly, but I need to go back to the cabin. Sitting here watching Julie isn't doing me any good. But back at the cabin…"

"You'll be alone. Sitting there all by yourself, brooding."

"Actually, I've got more hospital expansion plans I'd like to work on and I hesitate to say this because when I do you'll probably try and hold me to something I don't want to commit to, but I'm enjoying it. In fact, I'm enjoying it so much I think I may knock out the whole west side wall and expand emergency services out about halfway across the staff parking lot. It'll double the emergency-room space, and maybe even give us enough space to build a full-service trauma surgery." He pushed himself to his feet. "And, no, I'm not going to be your trauma surgeon."

"So says you," Rafe said, chuckling.

"So says me, emphatically," Jess responded. "That's not my thing anymore."

"Like living in Lilly Lake wasn't my thing anymore?" Rafe challenged.

"Aunt Grace always said I was the stubborn one, and she was right. I am. So don't hold your breath waiting for me to take up the scalpel, because you'll just turn blue and pass out. Now, if you'll excuse me, I'm going to go and thank your lovely wife for the hospitality, pack my things and move out." Supporting his weight with his cane, Jess headed toward the front door.

"Do you have feelings for her, Jess?" Rafe called after him.

Jess smiled. "I've still got things to sort out in my mind about Donna. But Julie...maybe I do. Or maybe it's just something from the past creeping in, messing up my mind. I don't know. It's not going to make any difference one way or another. Like they say, there's too much water under that bridge."

"So why not build a new bridge and see what happens?"

Why not? He could think of at least a dozen reasons, and each of them began with *Julie deserves better.* She did. She absolutely did.

It was probably the worst thing she could be doing under the circumstances, but Rafe had been called into the hospital for an emergency surgery, so there was no one else available to take Jess home to his cabin except Edie, and she was busy with Molly. So Julie had said yes. It was late, anyway. Time to put Ghazi back in his stall, then go home. So the detour didn't matter. But she was nervous in any case, because of what had happened between them. More than that, because of what she'd finally admitted to herself.

The thing was, if she truly wanted to live in Lilly Lake again, she was going to have to get used to running into Jess from time to time. He did come home occasionally. And he was part owner of the hospital in which she worked. So maybe they wouldn't exactly be tripping all over each other, but those occasional bumps wouldn't be avoided. This evening was going to be one of those bumps. It was a short ride, however. And perhaps she and Jess could get things back on track. Or, at least, find their spot in the middle. Friends, acquaintances, two ships passing in the night, whatever. "Your foot feeling better?" she asked, holding open the car door for him.

"Swelling's gone down, so next time I stick my foot in my mouth it shouldn't be so bad."

She laughed. "Can we just get past...well, whatever it is that's making us do stupid things?"

"Kissing you wasn't stupid," he said as she shut the car door.

Outside, Julie walked slowly to the driver's side, hoping the heat of the flush creeping into her cheeks wasn't turning her bright red. No, kissing him hadn't been stupid. It had been more than stupid. It had been a disaster. One huge catastrophic event that had caused her to lose sleep. "So, I'm assuming you have sufficient food back at your cabin to tide you over for a couple days, since you won't be driving."

"Shouldn't we talk about it?" he asked.

"Your food situation?" Dreadful evasion. Her mind wasn't racing fast enough to change the subject to anything that made sense. In fact, she was so nervous she was on the verge of babbling.

Jess didn't reply to her inane response to him. Rather, his body language went rigid, and he folded his arms across his chest. Folded them *severely,* Julie noted out of the corner of her eye. Well, maybe it was for the best. This whole state of affairs between them was going from marginally okay to bad, and she wasn't sure there was a way to make it better, or even fix it a little bit. And even if they could fix it in the present, the past couldn't be fixed so easily, if at all. So, there they were. Two people flirting with feelings that wouldn't be realized. Feelings best avoided.

She sighed heavily and resigned herself to a quiet ride out to Jess's cabin. Almost like a couple of strangers. And so it went for a few minutes, until they were sitting in front of the cabin. Then Jess finally spoke. "Would it be easier for you if I went back to the city? You're the one trying to make a life for yourself here, and I'm the one who's only passing through from time to time. I want to make this easier for you, Julie. Which means that if what it will take is me going back to the city right now, that's what I'll do."

"No, don't. We need to figure out how to make this work between us. And right now I think it's good that you and Rafe are getting closer. I'd feel terrible if my being here was the reason you couldn't."

"But we're caught in a bad place, Julie. Can't go back, can't go forward."

"Maybe we don't have to *go* anywhere," she said, even though she knew that could never be the case between them. Not after that kiss.

"Or maybe we do," he said, almost as an afterthought as he climbed out of the car, shut the door and hobbled up to his cabin.

She thought about stopping him. Thought about getting out of the car and asking him what he meant by that, but she knew the answer. Their unfinished business was so thick that it was an entity unto itself. Thick, and curdled, she thought as she turned the car around in his driveway and headed back to her house. But she didn't get far. Just a few hundred feet down the road, she jammed on her brakes. This wasn't the way she wanted to live, always straddling the tentative edge. Teetering, yet never falling. Jess was the only one who'd ever made her feel so...unsure, and she had to put an end to it. Move on emotionally, once and for all. Or stay, and be honest with him about how she felt. So rather than taking the time to turn the car around again and risk losing the momentum of her new found conviction, Julie hopped out and ran the short distance back to Jess's front door. Once there, she paused to take a deep breath, and without thinking looked in his window before she knocked.

She saw him there, standing in front of his fireplace, holding a picture of...it had to be Donna. His shoulders were slumped, he had the look of a man dejected. Maybe a man in love who still grieved his loss. Transfixed, she continued watching for a moment, looking through the glass as he sat the picture back up on the mantel, then backed away, stopped and looked at it again.

"This is crazy," she whispered. "He still loves her." Which was why he'd told Rafe he'd never do it again…never get involved in that way. In Jess's heart, there was only one woman. Julie knew that now. Had her answer even before she'd made her confession. So rather than knocking, Julie backed away from the window, then turned, ready to run down the three wooden steps and straight to her car. But before she'd touched foot on the first step, Jess opened the cabin door.

"Something wrong?" he asked, looking clearly puzzled over finding her there. "I thought you'd gone."

"I, um…I decided I should come back and see if I could fix you something to eat. With your foot and all, you need to get off it, prop it up, get some rest. So, um…" She shrugged. "Food. Can I do that for you?"

Jess chuckled. "You really do have a fixation, don't you?"

"Just the nurse in me."

He stepped back. "Well, never let it be said that I tried to quash the nurse in you. I don't have a lot in the way of groceries, but if you can find something that will assemble into a passable meal, you're welcome to have at it. As long as you stay and eat with me."

Hesitating a step before she entered, Julie squared her shoulders and braced herself. For what, she didn't know. Maybe just a pleasant couple of hours with Jess, maybe the most nerve-racking two hours she'd ever spent in her life. Either way, she hated being so indecisive. Wished she had Grace to talk to. Grace had always known what to do in any situation. While she'd never really told you what to do, she had always been a gentle guide, or a not-so-subtle push in the right direction, whichever method you needed.

Right now, she sure did need a push or a guide. "Look, Jess, I did..." She swallowed hard, caught herself staring at the photo on the mantel. Donna in full military uniform looking like the kind of woman Jess should have been with. "She was beautiful," she said. "Donna...I'm assuming that is Donna."

"She did turn a few heads," he said, on his way to an overstuffed easy chair in front of the window. "You don't mind if I sit down, do you?"

In answer, Julie scooted a foot stool underneath his leg once he was down. "Did you two meet in the military?" she asked, backing away from him.

"She was my superior officer, actually. I had the rank of captain, she was a major." He smiled fondly. "Her first order to me was to drop and give her twenty push-ups."

Julie laughed. "You were insubordinate?"

"A little bit. I saw her from behind. Let's just say that I admired the view, and made a comment to that effect. When she turned around… Pure fire in her eyes. I knew I was in trouble, especially when I saw that she outranked me." He chuckled. "And she was so cool, dishing out my punishment. She simply pointed to the floor and said *'Twenty.'* There was no mistaking what she meant."

"But you challenged her, didn't you?"

"You know me that well?" he asked, settling back into his chair.

"Well enough. And I'll bet it didn't take Donna long to figure you out either."

"She said pretty much the same thing."

"So, what was your punishment after you challenged her?"

"Twenty push-ups, followed by bedpan duty. I got to clean them when I wasn't on duty in surgery." He grinned. "A nice little lesson in humiliation."

"Bedpans…" Julie laughed so hard her side ached. "I'd have loved seeing that. You cleaning all those…"

Laughing, too, he held up his hand to stop her. "Every day for three days. She called it teaching me my lesson."

"Any woman who can have her way with you like that…"

He cleared his throat, breaking the direction of the conversation. "I, um…I have some more ideas for the expansion, if you'd like to go over them now."

"The expansion?" Such an abrupt change in conversation caught her off guard. Told her something she needed to know. Told her that it was time to let go of everything concerning Jess. The past, the fantasy. The back and forth feelings she was having. Time to get rid of all of it. Jess was where he wanted to be, and she wasn't included. "Oh, you mean the hospital."

"I want to turn the emergency room into a whole trauma unit...trauma beds, trauma surgery. I know you were working on plans to expand existing services, but the hospital needs to go beyond that. We can turn ourselves into the major hospital in the region for all kinds of trauma with a little extra effort. So..." He stood, then wandered over to his desk, punched a few computer keys and turned the screen toward Julie. "Interested?"

Once her head spun back to the place it should be, she glanced at his work. "That's a lot more than I thought it was going to be. Makes my contributions seem pretty insignificant."

"Your contributions are what got me to this." He turned off the screen, then plopped down in the desk chair. "Lilly Lake needs more. Rafe and I can do that, and we've decided we want to."

"But you're not staying once you're all better, are you?"

"That's right. I'm not. But that doesn't stop me from taking over this project. I want to do that,

Julie. Want to see what I can do to make the expansion something that will benefit everyone."

Which mean she was phased out. "It's your hospital," she said, trying to hide her disappointment. "I think if you want to invest in an expansion like what I imagine you're considering, then go for it. It would be a welcomed improvement."

"So why the frown?"

Julie shrugged. "I think I'm a little overwhelmed." Total lie. She was hurt. Didn't like being pushed aside. Wasn't going to show him he still had the power to hurt her so badly. "Going from an improved emergency department to what would amount to a little hospital inside a hospital…it's not what I'd expected. That's all."

"Your duties would be different."

"My duties?"

"As head nurse in the region's major trauma unit." He grinned. "Sounds like Julie Clark kind of responsibilities to me."

"Except I'm just out of school. Not experienced enough to manage something so…comprehensive."

"Sure you are. You have more trauma experience than most. And your management skills…

Wait. You don't think you're getting pushed aside, do you, Julie?"

She laughed nervously. "I don't know what I'm getting, Jess. With you, it's up and down, something different every minute."

"It's still all yours. A blank canvas to do with as you see fit. That hasn't changed."

"Hasn't it? Because it seems like everything has changed."

"In scope maybe. But not in intent. And you're part of the intent, Julie."

For sure, it was a lot to think about. She was flattered, though. And honored Jess had all that trust in her. More than anything else right now she was nervous, thinking about his expectations, because he was trusting her more than anybody else ever had. No sane hospital administrator or owner would ever hire someone as inexperienced in trauma as she was to run what she believed Jess was about to create. Sure, a small emergency room was one thing. But this whole expansion to a major trauma unit? "Shall I get cooking?" she asked.

"Don't worry about that, I have frozen dinners. How about I pop them in the microwave while you sit here at the computer, look at my notes and add your initial thoughts to them?"

"Are we still doing this together, Jess? The expansion?"

"Can you stand me long enough to do it?"

Pushed aside, not pushed aside…she wasn't sure which one caused the largest upheaval in her vacillating emotions. "How about I scrounge up a proper meal in the kitchen while I think about it, and we'll brainstorm ideas afterward if I decide to do it?"

"I never mean to hurt you, Julie."

"I know that." She did, too. But why did it always turn out that way? That was the question she pondered, along with her food prep, for the thirty minutes it took her to put a decent meal on the table. Chicken, vegetables, rice…emotions out of control. A few hopes creeping in. Hopes clouded by so much guilt.

"I didn't know you could cook," Jess said after his first bite. "It's good."

"Just stir-fry. I'm not exactly a domestic goddess, and I think anybody could do this." She stirred through the food on her plate, but didn't lift a bite to her mouth. "Look, Jess. I really need to get going. This was a bad idea...doing dinner."

"Doing it right now, or doing it ever?" He reached across the table and squeezed her hand. "We should have been smarter back then, Julie. Both of us. But we weren't, and that's making right now awkward."

"Well, we can't change the past, can we? And for what it's worth, you had a right to hate me. I hated myself for a long time afterward."

"Because you thought you were pregnant?" He shook his head. "You were honest. You told me you weren't. And the last time I counted, there were two of us involved in all that, Julie. So I didn't hate you, couldn't hate you. But my old man..."

"I saw what he did, Jess. Saw what he did to your horse because of me. I was there that day, and I felt so bad because I'd known for a couple weeks that my pregnancy was a false alarm. But I was still wrapped up in some stupid fantasy. Then after I saw him kill Storm, and watched you take the shovel to him, I realized that if I'd told you sooner he wouldn't have killed Storm and you wouldn't have come so close to killing..."

She drew in a quivering breath. "I'm so sorry for that, Jess. I was so wrapped up in my own little world, it never occurred to me that something like that could happen. And maybe, in some small way, what you said was true. Maybe I was trying to think of a way I could trap you. Not that I would have, in the end. But I did wonder what would happen if I simply didn't tell you I wasn't pregnant. But then after your father…"

She swallowed back a lump in her throat. "I understood why you left, Jess. I deserved it, probably even caused it, and I deserved everything you said." She pulled her hand from his and pushed herself back from the table. "I had nightmares for months. And I was so afraid that if Grace knew I was the reason you left she'd want me gone."

"We were kids. Kids do, and say, dumb things."

"But that's not an excuse. Look what happened because of me. You loved that horse, Jess. I saw your pain, pain that you had to go through because of me."

"Because of my old man, Julie. He's the one who killed Storm, not you."

She shook her head. "It was my fault he got to that place." She swiped away a tear sliding down her cheek. "And I'm so sorry. Can you ever forgive me?"

"There's nothing to forgive."

"How can you say that, Jess? You're a mess, I'm a mess. I'm walking on eggshells because I don't want to…"

"What, Julie? You don't want to what?"

"Make the same mistake twice. I like this new life. Love it. So I have to know that if we do work together on this project, this life I love isn't going to be taken away from me because of our…history. We're crazy right now. Both of us. And that kiss…it just opened too many old wounds. I can't do that. Won't do that."

He raised an eyebrow. "Well, I've got to give you credit for one thing. You're honest."

"I have to be, Jess. Look what we've done to each other in the past."

"In the *past*," he reminded her.

"But the past is going to repeat itself if we're not careful. *And you know that!* Look at the circles we're going in, you confused over Donna, me confused over you. That's how it started the first time, both of us confused over so many things in our lives. So you can't kiss me again, Jess. Can't do…anything. Or I'll leave Lilly Lake. That's my decision." Brave words. Truth was, close proximity to Jess scared her to death, no matter how brave she sounded. This was where it had to truly end for them.

So, she did leave. Carried her plate to the kitchen and continued walking straight out the door, feeling sad for all the things that never had never been. Not angry. Not even hurt. Just very, very sad. But so was Jess. And there really was no going back for them. No going forward either, except as friends, colleagues and partners in hospital business. She and Jess, though…they would have made beautiful babies together. Unfortunately, life had moved on, and they'd both been swept away to other places.

Still, for a moment, she could almost see herself with a baby in her arms. Their baby. Almost…

CHAPTER EIGHT

LIKE the old saying went, the night wasn't fit for man or beast. Only tonight it had started in a deluge, one predicted as slight showers, then had gone horribly wrong after that. Jess stood at the front door, filling up the frame with his broad shoulders, watching her debate whether or not to make a run for it or simply tuck herself away on the porch swing and wait it out. "You're really not going out in that?" he asked, when it became apparent that was her decision.

"It's just water. I'll get wet, I'll dry." Truth was, she really didn't relish the idea of going out there. But given the choice between that storm and the storm she felt around Jess, the lightning and thunderstorm seemed the better option. "Not a big deal."

"If the road washes out, it will be," he warned, keeping his distance.

"Look, I'll be fine, Jess. Besides, I'm not going

straight home anyway. I need to stop by the stables and see how the horses are doing before I leave. We've got a few in there who are going to spook pretty badly in the storm, and someone needs to make sure they're doing okay. You know, get them settled in, calmed down."

"Let Johnny take care of them."

"He's at his daughter's this evening. Over in Jasper. He just texted me to see if I could get by and look after the horses, and I said I would." Actually, she'd texted him and volunteered. It was her quickest way out of the cabin, and away from Jess. Being anywhere near him confused her, and she needed to keep a clear head.

"Well, if you have to go to the horses, then I'm going with you."

She pointed to his foot. "With that? I don't think so."

He held up his cane. "With this."

"No! I can't let you do that, Jess. First off, Rafe would kill me. He ordered you off that foot for a few days, and even though you seem to be getting along fine, I'm not going against his orders. Second, I don't need your help out there. I'm just going to have a look at a few skittish horses and calm them down if they need it. And if the storm gets any worse than it already is, I'll spend the night in the stables. I'll be fine. You don't have to worry about me." She walked over to the edge of the steps, then looked back at him. "One thing I've learned over the years is how to take care of myself. Started doing it when I was young, and haven't stopped. And I'm good at it, Jess. Better than most. Even in the rain." *And through the tears she wanted to hide in the rain.* With that, she stepped off the porch and started to run to her car. But halfway there, she heard Jess shouting at her. So she looked back, only to find him making his way in her direction…limping, dodging ruts, using his cane as a feeler.

"Jess, stop it! Go back!" she shouted at him as a clap of nearby thunder literally shook the ground underneath her. "I told you I don't want you coming with me!"

But he wouldn't do it. Wouldn't turn around. Which was exactly what she expected from him…that stubborn, pig-headed… "Jess!" she shouted again, when she noticed he was picking up his pace. She could outrun him, get to her car, get in and drive to the stables. And leave him standing there. But Jess was obstinate enough to walk that half-mile, which distressed her more than it frustrated her. Damn him, anyway. He knew he shouldn't be doing this! Yet here he was, the quintessential Jess Corbett, on the path to another huge risk. "Why can't you listen to anybody?" she shouted at him. "You do these stupid things, take all these risks… Jess, it's crazy."

His answer was to pause for a moment, then shrug. "Someone has to."

"No, they don't, Jess! That's just it. Putting yourself at risk unnecessarily doesn't help anybody. It makes them worry…makes *me* worry. And if people are worrying about you, how can you expect them to do the things they need to do? Like Rafe? He's in emergency surgery right now. What if he knew that you're out here, getting ready to do God only knows what? How's that going to affect him in surgery, if he has to worry about you?"

"But he doesn't *have* to worry about me."

"If that's what you think, then you're just being blind. Of course he has to worry about you. So does Edie, and Molly. So do I. It goes with the territory…you know, family and friends. That's what it's about, Jess, whether or not you want to admit it. You are part of this little Gracie circle of people, so that concern is going to come right at you! And because of that, you've got to take your actions into consideration and realize how they affect other people. I mean, what you're doing right now…it's stupid, considering your condition."

"Maybe it is, but those are my horses out there," he shouted back over the noise of the thunder rumbling in closer by the minute. "And there's nothing wrong with me. There wasn't when I was given a two-week *time-out* to rest, and there wasn't when Rafe taped up my foot. I'm fine." He reared back and threw his cane as far as the eye could see, considering the weather conditions. "Just fine."

"Why are you doing this, Jess? Not just coming out in the storm this way, but everything? Why are you doing what you do? Is it because you feel guilty? Survivor's guilt, maybe? Donna died, you didn't? Because if that's the case…"

"You're right, I feel guilty about Donna, in ways nobody would ever understand. Or maybe they would if they know me. You know, Jess

Corbett being true to his nature, not bending an inch. Not even for the woman he loves. Well, I don't need counseling because of it. And I sure don't need everybody who's supposed to care about me standing off on the sidelines, looking concerned and trying to get me to change the error of my ways. I do what I want to do, because..." He shrugged. "You know what, Julie? I don't know why. Okay? I honestly don't know why. Maybe it's just who I am, who I always was. Don't know, don't care. But what I do know is that instead of everybody trying to change me, they ought to just accept me for what I am and what I do. Life comes with risks and mine just seem...bigger. I'm not irresponsible, I don't have a death wish. I just...react. And I accept that in me." He swiped the rain off his face. "The one thing I'll do, though, is consider the people who care for me, and try to temper some of my reactions to make them—*you*—feel easier."

She scrambled after his cane, then brought it back to him. Had Donna been at odds with him over his actions? Because what she sensed coming from Jess wasn't survivor's guilt so much as something much deeper. Something much more paralyzing. "I think that's all anybody has ever wanted, Jess. Not to change you but to make you realize that they—*we*—are part of who you are and what you do. You don't do these things alone. We do them with you. Just recognize that."

His expression softened. "You know we're better than friends, don't you?"

"I don't know what we are, Jess."

"When you included yourself in that circle of concern for Jess Corbett, you knew."

She wouldn't dispute him on that. She'd always known who they were, and that was the problem. "Just think about the people who care. That's all I'm asking. That, and would you please just go back to the cabin and let me handle the horses?"

He chuckled. "You know, I really like the way you can take a simple conversation and turn it around without missing a beat. The thing is, you're quick to point out just how stubborn I am, but you've got a good case of it going yourself. And you do need help, Julie! Even though you won't admit it, even hate to admit it...you've always been like that, by the way... Anyway, you may be able to take care of *yourself* without any help, but you can't take care of those horses by yourself. Not in this storm!"

She hated that he knew her so well. At the same time, though, she liked it. It was to no avail, of course. Their time had come and gone, and it wasn't going to get a replay. Yet knowing that he could anticipate her like he did gave her back a little bit of the sixteen-year-old girl who'd loved falling head over heels in love with Jess. "There's nothing I can say to change your mind?"

"Like I said, you're not doing this alone. Not tonight, not under these conditions. I'm not walking away from you this time, Julie."

I'm not walking away from you this time... She wasn't exactly sure how to take his words, and for most of the short ride down to the stables she tried not thinking about them, tried not to attach any particular significance or interpretation. But each time she allowed them to float through her thoughts, her skin prickled, and her stomach churned. Because she knew what she wanted him to mean, and it was the same thing she didn't want him to mean.

But it had been her choice to come back to Lilly Lake. The thing was, she'd known what could happen, and she'd come anyway. That's probably what confused her more than anything. She'd walked right into it, then fought it every step of the way. But what was she really fighting? At this point, she didn't know.

"I think the storm's getting worse," Jess commented as they rounded the last bend before Gracie Stables, then stopped.

"Look, Jess. I'm going over to the main stable. I need to see what condition the horses are in there, then I'll take a look at what's going on in the other stable. Since you're going to work no matter what anybody says, would you see what's going on in here?" She referred to the smallest of the three stables where the younger horses were generally kept. "You know, figure out which ones need the most help? We've got a couple of babies in there, and I haven't been around long enough to know how they're going to do in this storm."

Jess swung himself out of the car, and stood there for a moment, simply looking at her, looking like he wanted to say something. But he didn't. Instead, he nodded a loose acquiescence then walked away without a word.

But what was there to say? He still loved Donna.

Maybe somewhere in all those conflicting emotions, they could salvage a friendship. Maybe they couldn't. And right now she just didn't have time to think about it.

"We didn't get them all in," one of the volunteers shouted from the far end of the stable. He was a young boy, not quite twenty. Wiry, but slight. And bent on a career in equine medicine. Bobby Lee Bright. "Storm came out of nowhere, and we were trying to get them all stabled, but we got caught off guard."

Now her nerves were on edge. Having horses out in a storm like this, especially horses in the delicate condition so many of them were, wasn't good. "How many?"

"Fifteen. One I'm particularly worried about. We couldn't get her rounded up, and she's totally spooked...she's coal black, no name yet."

She knew exactly which one. Poor thing had come in with lesions on her hindquarters and maggot-infected open sores on her front legs. Malnourished. Wobbly on her feet. And so sweet and loving with just the smallest amount of attention. Thinking about that horse scared to death out in the storm... Nothing else mattered. She had to get that horse in. "Who else do we have here to help us get them back?"

Bobby Lee came running up to her, out of breath. "Just Summer Adair. She's over in the pasture right now, trying to get the horses into the corral there. I did call a couple other people who are on their way, but right now it's just the two of us…three, including you."

Four, including Jess, who wasn't going to be counted out of this even though, in her opinion, he should be. "Okay, I'm going over to the pasture to see what I can do. You stay here, make sure everything's locked down tight, see if you can get a couple more people out here to help, because we're going to need to brush these horses down. Oh, and if you think we've got any horses that need medical attention, call the vet." She thought about Jess, and having him at her side right now would have been nice. "I'm going to stop at the small stable on the way over to the pasture, so radio Summer and tell her I'll be over there in a few minutes."

"You okay?" she called to Jess once she got to the smallest stable. He was making his way down the stable row, looking into each and every stall.

"I'm okay, but I've got a couple who are pretty badly spooked. I called Doc Halliday to come and sedate them or do whatever he thinks will get them through the storm the best way, so he'll be out here in a little while. How's everything else? All squared away?"

"No, it's not, Jess. We've got a problem…fifteen horses loose over on the pasture. Summer's trying to round up as many as she can and get them into the corral so we can bring them back across. One of the horses is critical, though, which worries me because she might bolt. So I'm on my way over there now. Got Bobby Lee in the large stable, taking care of things, and a couple people on their way in." She looked at the filly that was nuzzling Jess from behind. A spirited chestnut. "Do you have a horse of your own now?" she asked, as she started to gather up the equipment she needed…flashlight, rope, boots.

"Haven't had one of my own since Storm." Pulling a yellow rain slicker off a hook by the door, he shook his head. "I just ride whichever one Johnny tells me to take out."

The chestnut, a real looker with huge, soulful eyes and a very strong personality, nudged Jess forward so hard he stumbled right into Julie. Maybe it was time for Jess to change that, for him to make that particular break from his past. One step forward… "Well," she said, moving away from him enough to let him help her into the slicker, "I think you're being chosen."

He glanced back at the horse, then chuckled. "If that's the case, I think you should know that the one doing the choosing is named Julie."

Was that a double entendre, or did he simply mean the horse? "Her name's Julie? Did you just make that up?"

"Her name is Julie. Swear, that's what Molly called her." He pointed to Julie's hair just before she pulled a rain hat down over it. "Red hair color, and all. Molly said the chestnut reminds her of you, hence the name." He shrugged, smiled. "So you think Julie's choosing me?"

"I think the horse is choosing you."

"Only the horse?"

Now she was flustered. Didn't know how to respond even if she could have gotten the words out of her mouth. "Look, when I have time, I'll stop by the house and thank Molly for naming the horse after me. In the meantime..."

"In the meantime, just relax, Julie. Okay? We've got some things to figure out, but later."

Things, like his feelings for Donna? Or how he'd said he didn't want to do that again? Too many things, as far as she was concerned. Too many big things that could otherwise be defined as obstacles. All that going against her feelings... And he thought she could relax? "The only thing we have to figure out is how to get those horses back over here as quickly as possible."

Jess handed her a radio as she brushed past him on her way out the door. "You don't need to be the one going out there by yourself to get those horses."

She shrugged it off. Actually felt pleased he was concerned for her. Felt anxious, too, just to get away from him. "It's not a big deal. And it's probably easier than what you're going to have to do to dry the horses once we get them back over here. I'm worried about pneumonia, since a few of those horses aren't in the best physical condition. Until Doc Halliday gets here, you're the one who'll have to take care of that."

"And I'm worried about you," he said, grabbing her by the yellow lapels and pulling her over to him. "This would be the place where I'd kiss you…a nice, circumspect kiss on the forehead. But I won't. I want you to know that's what I'd be doing right about now, though."

"Isn't telling me you'd be kissing me pretty much the same thing as kissing me?" she asked, feeling even more flustered.

"Trust me, telling and doing are two different things altogether."

Hiding her confusion, she pushed him back. "Save it for the *other* Julie, okay?" Then, before he had a chance to respond, a chance to break down her barriers yet again, she turned and ran to the paddock across the road, never once slowing down, never once looking back. Even though she could feel him watching her.

"She's pulled up lame," Summer called from across the corral once Julie got over there. She was referring to a filly called Fancy, named for the number of pretty markings on her, all of them different. "Got spooked and jumped the corral. I think it might be a bowed tendon. She was already back at the knee to begin with, so it makes sense." Back at the knee referred to an equine condition where the horse's knee was offset so as to let the knee hyper-extend or bend backward.

Julie stopped, looked at the filly, who was standing off a way, looking at her. "Jess is in the front stable, and he's expecting the doc any time. See if you can take Fancy in there before she hurts herself any more."

"I'm not sure you should be over here by yourself. I mean, I know you're one of the foundation volunteers, but…"

Julie held up her hand to stop her. "I grew up here. Lived in Gracie House, know my way around a horse."

Summer laughed. "You're *that* Julie? Grace mentioned your name, but I never made the connection."

"I'm *that* Julie."

"Then I turn the literal reins over to you. And I'll send someone back to help you as soon as I have someone to send." With that, she spun away, and started to make her very slow way over to Fancy, who seemed to back away with every movement Summer made.

Julie watched for a moment, then turned into

the wind and pushed through it to get to the other side of the corral where several of the horses were standing together in a clump. Every step of the way, advancing three steps forward and getting blown one step back, she thought about how Jess's physical strength would have been a huge help right now. Help she would have loved. But his moral support was what she needed most. The kind of strength that would brace her in more ways than physically. Important ways.

However, she could still envision the look in his eyes when he'd stared at Donna's photograph…a look that had betrayed his true heart. It wasn't anything she could compete against. Nothing she wanted to either.

"Doc's going to stay in the stable," Jess yelled, coming up behind her. Like Julie, he was dressed in a yellow rain slicker, with a rain hat pulled low over his face. Looking like he was ready to be out in the pasture, he wore mud boots and carried a flashlight in one hand, with a rope coiled around his shoulder.

"You can't be out here. Your foot…"

"This is what I do," he said, catching up to her. "I rescue. And my foot's fine enough."

"Jess, we've still got fourteen horses to lead out of the pasture. Fourteen, after Summer gets hold of one we've got hurt. That's a lot of work…"

"Seven for you, seven for me," he said, actually going ahead of her by several steps. Then he stopped, turned back and held out his hand for her. "Are you with me?"

"I'm with you," she said, taking hold of his hand. "But, Jess Corbett, if you so much as grimace or wince, I'm going to tie that rope around you and drag you back to the stables myself. Understood?"

She was so cute when she was taking charge. "Understood." Somewhere close by, a bolt of lightning split the sky, followed by an almost immediate boom of thunder, which caused one of the horses to spook and sail over the pasture corral fence, then head straight down the road. The horse was running in blind fear, and the outcome wouldn't be good for it if they didn't get it back. Soon. He knew that, and from the expression he saw on Julie's face, she knew it, too. But they had other horses… "We'll get him later," he promised, coming up on the fence, still holding onto Julie's hand.

"Her. It's a filly. Came to us in bad shape... parasites, pronounced muscle weakness, eye infection. Hope you're right, that she'll come back. We haven't had her too long, 'though I think she oriented to the pasture pretty well. But in a storm like this..."

A storm like this was always the question, wasn't it? He hoped the filly would come back, but in reality he feared that was just wishful thinking. On a night like this, a spooked horse could run for hours. Exhaust itself. And a horse that wasn't in good shape to start with...well, he wasn't about to say or suggest anything negative to discourage Julie. She wore her heart on her sleeve for these animals, and he knew just how much that heart caused her to want to run down the road after that horse. So if thinking that the horse would come back on its own made her feel better, that's what he wanted her to think.

Another crash of the thunder sent three of the horses to charging the corral fence, but before they could injure themselves, Julie hopped over and literally waved them back into the center of the area. Arms flapping, she ran directly toward them, shouting at the tops of her lungs. "Back!

Get back!" she yelled, running in a zig-zag pattern to make sure she was being seen by the horses. Jess, on the other hand, entered the corral through the gate and immediately lassoed the largest of the three panicked horses, then started to pull him back toward the gate.

"Good rope skills," Rick Navarro called from out of nowhere. "Rafe's still tied up in surgery, so I thought I might be of some use out here."

"Thanks," Jess said. "Don't get to use them much lately. Nice to know I can still hold my own, bad foot and all. Look, Rick…"

Rick held up his hand to stop him. "As far as I'm concerned, we're good. Okay? The past is the past, and we've all made our share of dumb mistakes."

"Some dumber than others."

Rick chuckled. "You're right about that."

"At least let me say the words. Maybe you don't need to hear them, but I need to say them. And I'm sorry. All the things I said, all the things I did… We bullied you and you didn't deserve that. No excuses. What we did was wrong. Rafe and I…we both have a lot of regrets but I want you to know that you're one hell of a hospital chief of staff, and I consider myself fortunate that you've decided to stay with us in spite of how Rafe and I treated you."

"We all grow up," Rick commented, extending a hand to Jess. "And learn from our mistakes."

"And learn from our mistakes," Jess repeated, taking Rick's hand. "Some of us with more mistakes than others. So, how about we see what we can do to get some of these horses back across to the stable? Since I'm not so fast on my feet right now, Julie and I can round them up here and you can lead them back across."

"That I can do. But there's going to be a cost involved," Rick replied, as one particularly rambunctious stallion caught his eye. The horse was literally scoping out the fence, getting ready to charge and keeping an eye on Rick at the same time.

"Whatever you want. Name it."

"A horse for me...maybe that wild-eyed chestnut over there." He pointed to the horse that was watching him, challenging him. "And a gentle one for my son."

"Small price to pay. Glad to do it," Jess said,

slowly stepping away from Rick. "So let's see if we can get that chestnut right now. Okay?"

"Okay by me," Rick said, keeping himself in full view of the horse while Jess edged his way behind it and roped it, one attempt all slick and tidy, like he was a rodeo cowboy. Then handed the rope over to Rick.

Over the next little while, volunteers wandered in and, amazingly, all the horses were brought to safety within half an hour. Little by little, they were being dried, then checked by Doc Halliday. It was a sight to behold, Jess thought to himself as he stood back and watched the people show up and simply throw themselves into the work. Some were Gracie Foundation volunteers who worked regularly with the horses. Others were merely people who had responded to the call for help that had gone out from the hospital. People he knew, people he'd yet to meet. Rick was squarely in charge of the group, too, a natural leader without even trying. Jess liked the man, was glad they'd put aside differences. Rafe was right about him. Rick did need to be brought in as their third partner. That's the least he could do. That, and a couple of horses.

Also, he could see why Rafe had decided to stay in Lilly Lake. Get away from the malignant memories of the old man, and it really wasn't such a bad place. Rafe was happy here now. But that was Rafe.

Could *he* be happy here, too? Because part of him really wanted to be. And part of him was scared to death of what he'd do with that happiness if he ever let it in. Which part, though, would win out if it came down to a battle? Because every time he looked at Julie, he felt the battle brewing.

CHAPTER NINE

IF ANYTHING, the weather was getting worse. The brute force of the storm seemed to have doubled, and what should have been a fairly easy walk down the private road separating the two properties—the Gracie property and the land where Jess and Rafe's family home had once stood—was anything but. In fact, each step was more labored than the one before, and it was all Julie could do to keep herself upright. If not for the fact that the wind blowing back against her was so hard, she'd have probably toppled straight over face-first in the mud. Thankfully, as the wind fought against her, it was also helping her stay upright. With great effort, though, as the wind's intent was clearly to knock her over.

Had Jess discovered her missing yet? She hoped not. He didn't need to be out in this, and he would have been trudging along with her, shoulder to shoulder, if he knew where she was. More than that, she didn't need him anywhere near her right now, as the more they were together, the more she wanted to stay near him. Like an addiction. That addiction, topped by a whole boatload of confused feelings...even some solitary time in the thick of the storm was a welcome relief as she needed to do so some substantial sorting out. But how did anybody even begin to sort something like this?

Of course, there was the possibility that she was simply stalling or putting off the inevitable, that this whole situation with him would never work. Or maybe she was just plain scared to read ahead to the ending. Definitely too many confused feelings to make sense of right now. On top of that whole mess, Jess had his own set of problems going. He was larger than life, a man who laid down his own terms and didn't sway after that... always had been like that. That's why she'd been so drawn to him when they'd been kids. She'd felt safe with him. Why she was still so drawn to him. He walked his journey the way the man of her dreams would, which had made him a tough act to follow after he'd walked away from her. Or, in her case, impossible to follow, hence the lack of boyfriends, man friends, male relationships in her life…another part of her mess. Nobody lived up to Jess. Nobody came close.

Truth be told, she liked that quirk in him that pushed him to the edge, that made him do what others didn't dare. It's what made him real. And exciting. And so attractive. It's also what scared her the most because she understood it, and to expect him to change that part of himself was to, in essence, diminish him, to make him less than he was. So those were feelings she had to deal with, too, which was why she needed time away from him where his mere presence wasn't influencing her. Even if it was time spent in what was being called the worst storm Lilly Lake, New York, had experienced in more than a decade.

So she'd ducked out, hopefully unnoticed, as everybody hurried to dry off the wet horses. Jess included in that. Naturally, by now she was hoping she'd have found the filly, affectionately called Fugitive, and be on her way back to Gracie Stables before anybody missed her. She was scared to death for that horse, wouldn't rest until…well, optimally, Fugitive was brought back safe. Unfortunately, the farther she trailed on in this mess, the more discouraged she was getting. There were no signs of a horse coming this way, no tracks in the mud, no nothing. Not that she was able to see much at all. In addition, the beam from her flashlight was beginning to flicker, meaning low batteries, meaning no light in a matter of minutes. So she kept it shut off and fought her way on down the road, her discouragement as thick as the mud in which her boots were sticking.

Twenty minutes into her search, Julie squelched off the road to catch her breath. Her lungs and legs burned, she had a headache, her jaw hurt from clenching it so tight. And now she was beginning to wonder if she should give up the search and try again in the morning, after the storm had passed through and daylight would definitely be on her side. It was a plausible idea, even a good one. But every time she thought about that sweet horse out in this, lost, scared… Somebody'd rescued *her* once, when she'd been out there lost and scared in a so-called storm of her own making, and that's the thought that carried Julie right back up to the road to continue on. Except this time, before she even pushed herself forward into the storm's wall, something caught her attention. A light in the distance? Someone coming up the road behind her? Or maybe just the reflection of some distant lightning?

Julie stopped, looked. Sure enough, it *was* a light, and she knew whose. He was in a truck, catching her in the headlights. Slowing down once her image was framed in the beam, thereupon coming to a complete stop just a few yards away from her. "You're driving?" she yelled at Jess over the din of storm sounds. "You know Rafe told you not to."

Jess opened the truck door, then stepped out, grinned his notoriously engaging grin and put on an exaggerated shrug. "You thought I'd actually listen to him?"

Of course she didn't. If he had listened, he wouldn't be the Jess Corbett she...

"I thought you'd exercise some common sense," she replied before that thought took shape, approaching him.

"And *what* about bringing the horse trailer out to get a missing horse isn't common sense?"

She stepped directly into him, directly to a place where their faces were mere inches apart.

"The part where you're driving." Then she spun away and headed to the driver's side door.

He followed, smiling a smile she couldn't see. A different smile from his usual grin. A smile of insight. "Been doing it since I was ten or eleven. Or, for the sake of being legal, sixteen. So you're right. I'm driving. And you wouldn't have it any other way, would you, Julie? Let me rephrase that. Reverse our situations, where you're the one with the bad foot and I'm the one wandering around out here, looking for the horse. Would you have driven out with the trailer, against doctor's orders, to help me?"

She turned to face him, at once blocking him from getting near the driver's door. Sure, it was a test of wills. She knew that. But she also knew that someone had to set Jess straight, here and now. He was injured, and the nurse in her would have done no less for any other patient. Of course, the nurse in her wouldn't be having the sexy thoughts she was having for Jess. Admittedly, the sparring between them always was sexy, even in the middle of a horrendous storm. "Your point being?"

"One point, one fact. We're alike."

Well, she hadn't expected that. Didn't exactly want it, since alikes didn't attract. "If we are, then it's a good thing *opposites* attract," she snapped back, disappointed that he saw them being alike. Climbing up into the truck cab, she mulled over the reality. Opposite, alike… The thing was, they probably were alike. Grudgingly, she recognized it, wondered about it. Even worried that if opposites did attract, what could two alikes find for themselves, provided they ever got to the place they wanted to find something for themselves, long shot that it was? "So, are you getting in?" she yelled, more out of frustration than trying to be heard. "Or are you going to stand out here on the road and wait for me to come back for you later on?"

His grin reappeared. "You'd leave me here alone?"

"Yeah, I'd leave you here alone because I have a horse to find. My priority, Jess. My only priority." She slammed shut the truck door and rolled down the window. "You're slowing me up."

Jess chuckled. "Somehow, Julie, I don't think anything in life has ever slowed you up if you didn't want it to." Rather than going around to the passenger's side, though, he opened the driver's side door and swung himself up, effectively pushing Julie across the bench seat. "And before you say it, I'm fine to drive. Foot doesn't hurt… much."

"Doesn't hurt *much?*" she sputtered, wondering if she wanted to get out altogether or stay pressed up to him, where it felt so good. Pleasant memories were flooding back…the hard crush of his body to hers, the way her own body practically betrayed her every time Jess touched her. She was older now, but she felt that same sway of betrayal, even through several layers of soaking-wet clothes and two yellow rain slickers. Which made exiting the cab, *immediately,* the only sensible thing to do. Except nothing inside her was able to push her toward the passenger's door. Not one single scrap of willpower to be found in that truck .

"Didn't we already have this argument?" he asked. "You know. The one where you point out something that's for my own good and as much as I appreciate it, I'm too stubborn to take your suggestion."

His head was turned so that she couldn't clearly

see the grin on his face, but she could sure feel it burning a hole in her countenance. Feel it chipping away her defenses. "Apparently we didn't have it all the way to its logical end."

He laughed outright at that. "You mean not all the way to the end you want? And you call me stubborn?"

"I'm not stubborn so much as…"

"Inflexible?" he volunteered.

"Practical," she corrected. "You're injured, I want to drive because of that. That's being practical, Jess. So, is it that you don't trust my driving? Is that what this is about? Because I drove an ambulance in my early days as a medic. I can probably out-drive you on your best day, and the proof is in the lack of me having an injured foot and you having one because of a moment of bad driving." She sat back, crossed her arms over her chest in the self-satisfaction that she'd won this round, then tossed him a *bet-you-can't-top-that* grin. "Next argument?"

But he did top that, in a seriously provocative voice and an argument that couldn't be won. "What I don't trust, Julie, is me looking for the horse…not with something much nicer to watch sitting right next to me, distracting me. Which you will." Well, apparently, those were the words for which she didn't have a comeback. Words that were actually tingling all the way to her toes. Because Julie simply didn't respond. Couldn't respond.

"What? Nothing to say?" he teased. "Did I finally manage to say something for which you don't have a reply?"

"Oh, I have a reply," she lied, balling her trembling fists. Everything was trembling, arms, legs, lips…her heart. This was getting so dangerously close to being real, and she was surprised to find how unprepared she was for what she wanted. "Which will have to wait because we need to be concentrating on the rescue,"

"I'm a patient man, Julie. Willing to wait as long as I have to." He glanced into his rear-view mirror in preparation to pull onto the road, and saw what appeared to be a large flashlight beam coming down the road. "I think that's probably Bobby Lee," he said after several seconds. "He's really worried about the horse. I told him to stay back, but he's stubborn, like the rest of us."

Julie leaned across and opened the passenger's

side door for the boy, who was out of breath as he climbed in next to her.

"They spotted Fugitive about half an hour ago," he said, gasping. "She went right up to the front of Brassard's Pub, looked in the window like she wanted in."

Julie heaved a sigh of relief. "Then she's okay?"

"Yes and no. Several of the people ran outside to get her, and she spooked. Took off running in the direction of Sutter's Creek. Running fast, is what Will said. He chased her down on his motorcycle for a little way, but it was too muddy to go far, too dangerous. He'd heard we lost one, so he figured the filly was one of ours. Anyway, when he got to that big turn in the road, down by Trace Hollow, Fugitive took the path...the dirt path. Will decided not to go on because it's washing out in the storm. So he called."

"But it hasn't been that long," Julie said, trying to sound hopeful, even though she wasn't. "So we'll probably catch up with her, maybe where the path joins with the road again on the far side." A tediously long, dangerous trek.

"Or she'll head straight through the woods,"

Jess said. "Which means we won't be able to do much until morning."

"I'm not giving up," Julie said, her stubborn streak clearly showing.

"And I didn't say we would. But we have to be…what was the word you used a few minutes ago? Practical? We have to be *practical* about this." He reached over and squeezed her knee. "I want to get her back as much as you do, Julie. But I'm not going to let you risk hurting yourself to do it."

"So we give it another hour," she said.

"Then come back tomorrow if we don't get her," Jess added. "Come back *together*."

"But if we're going to give this another hour tonight, why don't you two drive back to the turn in the road?" Bobby Lee suggested. "Hopefully Fugitive hasn't strayed too far off that. In case she has, though, I'm going to take the shortcut on foot. She might double back to Brassard's, since she already knows that trail, and if she does, I can get her. So, one hour. If we haven't found her by then, we'll come back out at first light, with more people."

Julie looked out the truck windshield at what

seemed to be yet another storm front brewing. "It's getting worse again. I think you should skip the shortcut and ride with us, Bobby Lee."

He shook his head. "That's wasting time. And I'll be fine. I've taken that shortcut hundreds of times. No big deal." He clicked the handle of the truck door to open it. "See you at the turn."

In a way, he reminded her of Jess. Brave, stubborn... Nice catch for some girl someday. "Before you go, tell me why didn't you call us, instead of running down the road after us?" She held up her cell phone.

Bobby Lee grinned sheepishly. "Had to make a choice...new textbook or cell phone bill." Then he shrugged. "Grace was sort of helping me with the school expenses...she wanted me to come back to Lilly Lake as a vet and take care of her horses when I graduate. But after she died..."

Julie pressed her phone into his hand. "Take it. You can't be out there in this storm without being able to call in case...in case you find the horse before we do."

Bobby Lee tucked the phone into his pocket. "See you in a while."

After Bobby Lee was gone, and she and Jess

were on the road for Sutter's Creek, Julie still
sitting pressed to Jess's side, she asked, "Does
anybody even know how many people Grace
helped over the years, or was helping when she
died?"

"Not sure. I suppose if anybody knows, it would
be Henry Danforth."

"He was her lawyer, wasn't he?"

"And confidant."

"Do you think he'd tell us?"

"Does it matter?" Jess asked. "Aunt Grace
wasn't after any recognition, which is why she
didn't want people knowing what she did. She
was always afraid the city might erect some kind
of statue in her honor…" He laughed. "She called
it a pigeon roost. Said she didn't want to see herself immortalized with pigeons pooping all over
her head."

Julie conjured up that image, and laughed at
it. Yes, that was definitely what Grace Corbett
would have said. "You're a lot like her, Jess. Did
anybody ever tell you that?"

He shook his head. "No, I'm not. Not even
close."

"Sure, you are. When Grace saw the need, she

helped. The way you do. For her, it wasn't for the glory. It's just who she was, something she had to do. And it's who you are, too. Grace rushed in, you rush in. And you both save lives. Sure, in different ways. But it's the same thing. In fact, right now you're thinking about helping Bobby Lee, thinking about picking up where your aunt left off in getting him through veterinary school. Aren't you?"

"He's a good kid. He deserves a break…and a cell phone. And, yes, I'd like to see him be able to come back here and look after the horses. So why not help him? Aunt Grace thought he deserved it, and she was the best judge of character I ever knew. Maybe a little financial aid to make things easier for him and, when the time comes, some mentoring on the finer points of running Gracie Foundation. He'd be a natural for the job."

"And you'd be a natural helping Bobby Lee." Impulsively, she twisted in Jess's direction and kissed him on the cheek.

"What was that? A kiss?"

"An *exception* kiss."

"So those are allowed? I must have missed that part in the rule book."

"You can make light of it if you want, but she'd be proud of you, Jess. You're going to do a very nice thing for Bobby Lee."

"But she wasn't proud of me," he said, tapping on the high beams as the truck moved forward. "Not since I came home from Afghanistan and decided not to be a doctor. I think that broke her heart."

"You know that for sure?"

"She kept telling me I was wasting my talent, not taking advantage of the things I had in life. That I had more to give. That I was underestimating myself, or maybe she meant underplaying myself. I don't know which, and I never asked because I was just so…" He gripped the steering-wheel tighter.

"Angry?" she asked.

"That, and a whole lot of other things."

"You loved Donna. Losing her the way you did…"

He shook his head. "That wasn't what caused the changes in me. I couldn't save her. With all my medical training, in the end there wasn't anything I could do except hold her. She'd been shot…sniper fire." Slowing the truck, he pulled off to the side of the road, and sat there, listening to the squeak of the windshield wipers, watching the drops on the windshield be wiped away, yet trying to look through them before they were.

"It was never enough for me, Julie," he finally said. "No matter what I did, it was never enough. I always had this feeling inside me that there had to be more. And I don't mean it had anything to do with the guilt my old man heaped on me year after year. You don't get impervious to it, but you do get used to it. Then there was Aunt Grace who always...*always* told me he was wrong. The hell of it is, Rafe and I both went on to be doctors. I'm sure the psychiatric community as a whole would have something interesting to say about that, considering that's what the old man was, and I sure don't know how Rafe accounts for his choice...we never talked about it. But for me, I figured going into medicine was my way of showing myself that I was better than my old man, that I could do better than he did. I still had this...this emptiness, though. Couldn't shake it, didn't know how.

"The thing is, when I was in Afghanistan, that's when I started to feel like I was...suffocating.

That I wasn't doing enough. Then I met Donna and we clicked. It was fast, and pretty intense. Good chemistry, I suppose you could say. Then one day I woke up engaged to be married and everything changed. I was getting a new life. I was getting…everything. Truth was, I was happy for a couple of months. Donna was making plans… plans for things I honestly didn't know could ever happen in married life or a family situation. Aunt Grace was the closest thing I had to a mother, and she wasn't exactly the type to put on an apron and make brownies. But that's what Donna was turning into before my eyes."

"And it scared you?"

Jess shook his head. "It didn't scare me so much as it…crowded me. Somehow, I'd pictured an entirely different kind of life. One that wasn't so… involved. Or maybe just involved in a different way."

"How would that have worked, Jess?"

"Beats the hell out of me. But the more I thought about it, the more I came to understand something in myself. I couldn't be in a marriage, couldn't survive in a marriage with Donna. I loved her, but not the way she needed to be loved, and there wasn't a damn thing I could do to change that."

"So maybe you could have avoided the marriage certificate and just gone with the committed relationship. It works for a lot of people."

"Maybe, but the thing is, it was the commitment part I didn't want. All I could think of was coming home every day at five o'clock, settling in to a nice little dinner and an evening of television with Donna. That was her vision, but it couldn't be mine. It wasn't enough."

"Not even if you had children."

"Not even with children. And it's my lack, Julie. Wasn't Donna's. She knew who she was, knew what she wanted. I didn't."

"How did Donna react to all that when you told her?"

"She didn't react, because I never got around to telling her how I was feeling."

"You mean she died…" Julie bit off her words. "Oh, Jess. I'm so sorry you didn't get it resolved with her."

"That's it. I did, but not the way I should have." He shut his eyes, drew in a deep breath and leaned his head back against the truck seat. "I started pulling away from her weeks before she died. Nothing drastic. The first thing she noticed was that I stopped helping with wedding plans. Then I quit talking about our future. Didn't get involved in the house plans she was sketching. And every time she asked what was wrong, I told her it was just battlefield fatigue, that I was stressed out. See, I wanted to run, but this was the one instance in my life where there was no-where to run. So I suppose I was hoping for some kind of miracle to drop down on me and make everything all better. But it didn't. I kept pulling further and further away, and it just got worse. Coward that I am, I was thinking that she'd get tired of our relationship, and of me, and break it off."

"You're not a coward, Jess. I think you just didn't want to hurt her."

"That's true. I didn't. The thing is, Donna really did make my life better. I could see it, Julie! I could feel it. But it wasn't…wasn't enough for me. Or maybe I wasn't enough for it. I don't know."

"Maybe you were just being too hard on your-self."

"The way the old man was always hard on me?"

He shook his head. "I don't think so. Because I kept feeling this...this huge void inside me, even when Donna was making me feel better."

"But you lived a tough life with him, Jess. Nothing was ever normal for you, and maybe that's what scared you about Donna—she was offering you a normal life for the first time in your life."

"I'm not sure I ever believed I was worthy of it, or even wanted to be worthy of it." He turned to face Julie. "After she died, I overcompensated for that. I know it. In fact, I *know* that every time I do something someone else considers too risky. That's me, trying to prove to myself that..."

"That you're worthy, that what you're doing is enough?" Julie said gently. "Trying to fill up that emptiness you've always felt?"

"Something like that. And I know it doesn't make sense..."

"It does, Jess. You were playing it safe up until you met Donna because that's the only way you knew how to survive. It got you through all those years with your dad, and it was the starting point for you and Donna."

"It should have been the starting point for us.

Should have been. But I never got to that place. There was Donna, making all these plans, so excited by the prospect of our new life together. And there was me, pulling away, and trying to fake it when I couldn't get far enough away fast enough. Donna brought everything and I brought…nothing. And she couldn't fill me up, Julie. I know that sounds bad, but she couldn't fill me up."

"Did you ever try to end it with her?"

He sighed heavily. "I'd started to end it. Told her I had serious misgivings about how we were going to make the relationship work, that I didn't think I had it in me to be all the things she wanted me to be. I told her that when we got back to the States I wanted to take a break, go off somewhere by myself and think for a little while. Told her I wasn't ending it, just postponing it. She started to cry, of course, and asked me what she'd done to cause it. I told her it was me, all me. That I felt…dead inside. That nothing in my life fit.

"Naturally, that hurt her. It wasn't what I'd meant to do, but that's what I did anyway. Taken this very strong woman and made her…weak. All she wanted was confirmation that I'd get over it, that her life would be normal again, that everything we'd planned would still work out. But I couldn't give it to her. None of it. Not one single ounce of hope except that we'd talk later." His voice cracked. "If I live to be a hundred, I'll never forget how hurt she looked. It reminded me of you that day, Julie, when I walked away from you. History repeating itself."

She laid a sympathetic hand on his arm. "But you made it right with Donna after that, didn't you? Or even a little better after you talked? Please, tell me you did!"

Jess shook his head. "She was killed an hour later."

"Oh, my God! I'm so sorry, Jess. I...I don't know what to say."

"Do you know what it's like, going to sleep every night knowing that what you said might have been the reason she...?" He choked. "I distracted her, broke her heart then sent her straight into the battlefield."

"It was a war zone, Jess. You can't make what happened to Donna your fault. She was a medic who went out to bring back the wounded...under fire. What happened was a tragedy. It's a tragedy every day when someone dies in combat. But you weren't the one who killed her."

"Wasn't I?"

Drawing in a ragged breath, Julie scooted over in the seat and put her arm around Jess. But he shrugged it off.

"I don't need your sympathy!" he snapped.

"Well, you sure need something," she replied. "So tell me what it is."

"To be left alone. To live my life the way I want to and not have people watching me, worrying about me, getting involved with me."

"Too late for that. You're being watched already. And worried about. And from what I've seen, there are a whole lot of people already involved with you in one way or another."

Turning to look at her, "Why the hell do you even care, Julie? I push you away, you push me away. So why are *you* the one coming to my rescue?"

"You know, I've asked myself the same question more than once lately. Truth is, I don't have a good answer. Not one you'd believe. I mean, I could say something like that's just who I am, or I'm only doing what I was trained to do. But that's not it. So how about I say that it's because I loved you so much back then, and leave it at that?"

"You were too good for me back then," he said.

"Of course I was! One of my many flaws."

He pulled off her rain hat to stare at her rosy-cheeked, beautiful face. Then sighed heavily. "Why are you such an optimist? Here I've just told you what a bad person I am, and you're still coming to my rescue. I don't deserve that, Julie."

"Everybody has confidence in you, Jess. Including me. You're not a bad person just because you were having doubts about your relationship with Donna. It happens to everybody at one time or another. Unfortunately for you, the timing turned an uncomfortable situation into a tragedy. But that doesn't make you bad, and I have an idea you were very kind and gentle trying to let Donna down. You just don't want to see it because you're afraid of letting someone else down. You lived with the letdowns when you were a kid...your dad let you down, life in general let you down."

"I let myself down."

"No, you didn't. In fact, look how far you've

gone to get yourself away from the things that let you down…you're a doctor, Army surgeon, fire-fighter. What I think, Jess, is that you're afraid you're too much like your father. You project his characteristics into yourself, probably because you're afraid that's how you really are. Kind of like me when I was a kid, pushing people away first, before they pushed me. Maybe that's why you were pushing Donna. I don't know. But what I do know is that it's a self-defense mechanism. Strike first, before you are struck.

"Sometimes I think it's easier to defeat your-self than let someone, or something, defeat you. That's all you're doing now. Striking first. Defeat-ing yourself. Probably all you did with Donna. The thing is, I knew your father, Jess. Saw the awful things he did to you, and you're not at all like him. In fact, there's nothing in you that's like anything he was. When you walked away from me, we were dealing with childhood issues. It hurt me, it hurt you, we hurt each other, because you had your goals and I had my fantasies. But we were both wounded kids, Jess, reacting the way wounded kids would react. Then we scarred over and grew up."

"Some scars bigger than others," he said.

"Maybe so. It's just that you've never let anybody get close enough to help you with that scarring-over process."

"You mean someone like you?"

"Or Donna. Did you ever tell her about your childhood? She might have been a great support to you."

He shook his head. "There were a lot of things I intended to tell her, but never got around to. It's hard to live your life on a battlefield. And I suppose I lived under the delusion that most of us do, thinking there's always more time."

"But there's not. We only get this moment. Then, if we're lucky, we get the next one."

She scooted back to her side of the seat. "And like I keep telling you, you're being too hard on yourself…in every moment. Especially when the person you need most to talk you out of it isn't here anymore."

She was so wrong about that. The person he needed most was here, right now. And she was the only one who'd ever filled that void in him. *The only one.* So, how did he deal with that? Or did he even deal with it at all? One more thing to add to their heap of mistakes—that Julie had filled him in a way Donna never could. "Look, I think we'd better get on down to Sutter's Creek after that horse." Shifting the truck into forward, he pulled back onto the road, mad at himself for pretty much everything in his life. At his age, something should have resolved by now. Instead, it was more complicated than it had ever been before. This time, though, he was wiser. Julie was all that counted, and she was better off without him. He'd just have to make sure that was the outcome…Julie, *without* Jess.

CHAPTER TEN

"Over there," Julie whispered, almost too apprehensive to breathe. "I think the headlight caught her…" She pointed to a thicket just at the turn of the road. "And unless the truck spooks her, we might be able to just walk up to her. By now, she's probably pretty tired, so I'm hoping she's not so inclined to run away again." Julie glanced around, didn't see any signs of Bobby Lee yet. "I'm surprised he's not already here. Anyway, you go back and get the trailer ready for me. I'm going to try and approach her, and hopefully she'll respond to me."

"You know she will," Jess said, switching off the headlights. "They always do. Man and beast alike." He opened his truck door and slid gingerly into the mud, sucking in a sharp breath as the slight jolt sent a bolt of excruciating pain up his leg. "I think you're going to have to take the lead on this one."

"Your foot?" she whispered, opening her own door and slipping outside. At the same time, she reached underneath her rain slicker to her jacket pocket and grabbed hold of several sugar cubes. Always be prepared was what Grace Corbett had taught her. Tonight, Julie was praying that a handful of sugar was all it would take with the horse. What it would take with Jess, though…

"What is it they say about doctors making the worst patients?" Out of the truck, Jess walked around to Julie's side, using the truck as his support.

"They say that some doctors who don't follow orders need to be tied up for their own good." She watched him make his way slowly around the truck. "Getting worse?" she asked.

"And if I were to admit that I re-twisted my foot a while ago?"

"Then I shrug…" She shrugged. "Say, too bad. And figure you know enough to quit when you have to because I know if I say anything else, we'll just be wasting time we don't have. Even if my personal preference would be to have you go sit in the truck and take care of yourself."

Jess laughed. "You always have to get in the last word, don't you?"

"Only if my last word is the word you need to hear." She grabbed a coil of rope and slung it over her shoulder.

"And who would be the one to determine that?" he asked.

"Me," she said, smiling.

"Okay, while you're getting in your last word, I'm going to call for backup. If the filly runs off again, I'd like to have enough people close by that we don't have to spend tomorrow doing this all over again. Personally, I'm in the mood to go back, get out of these wet clothes, put my feet up and have myself a nice, hot cup of coffee."

An image of the two of them getting out of their wet clothes together flashed through her mind. Thankfully, it was a quick flash, come and gone in an instant. "Call Bobby Lee, too. If he's anywhere near here, he might be our best bet to chase her down if she runs."

"Grace did a good thing with you," Jess said before he went all the way back to the trailer.

"What do you mean?"

"Training you to the horses. You love them the

way she did and you honor her in taking care of them like you do."

"Thank you," she said, quite touched. "I think that's the nicest thing anybody has ever said to me." She turned away when he did, trying her best to focus on the filly hiding in a clump of bushes, maybe a hundred yards ahead of her. The thing about Jess, though, was that he was never out of her mind. Which made it doubly important that she focus now. She *had* to get this horse. Thank God the rain had reduced itself to a drizzle for the moment. She was crossing her fingers that it would stay that way, no thunder, no lightning, until Fugitive was safe in the trailer or back in the stable.

"Okay, sweetheart," she whispered, as she approached the bushes. "I know you're in there. I saw you hiding, and I don't think you've gone anywhere yet."

She listened for a rustle, heard nothing.

"I have something for you." Stretching out her hand in front of her, she opened it to let the horse smell the sugar. "Here it is, come get it."

Listening again, she heard a snort and quickened her pace, but not so much as to spook the filly.

"There's more where this came from, sweetheart," she said. "I have a whole pocketful." Ten more steps, then she paused. "And you can have it all. Promise." Ten more steps, then she stopped again. "But I'm going to need for you to meet me halfway." Because if she went into the thicket, the horse might panic, then run again and injure herself. Or, as much as Julie didn't want to think about this, *she* could get injured. "So, come on out now. Let me see you."

Wiggling her hand, she felt the sugar cubes starting to melt in the drizzle. It wasn't good, as she had only another handful left. Consequently, she had to make this count. One way or another, it was time to make *everything* count. "We're getting down to the real deal here," she said to the filly. "Time to quit playing the game and do what you need to do." The same could be said of her life, couldn't it? Time for her to quit playing the game, time for her to do what she needed to do. And if Jess wasn't at that same place, and she was pretty sure he was not, well…she wasn't sure what would happen then. Wasn't sure what Jess would or would not do. But life was too short to waste wondering when you could be trying.

With Jess, she wanted to try, even though she was pretty sure he'd do some pushing for a while. This time, though, she wasn't a kid. Her total involvement with Jess wasn't a fantasy world. If anything, the roots of realty were so deep they weren't going to be easily pulled out or tossed away. In other words, she'd wait, if that's what she had to do. Wait, and let those roots hold her where she wanted to be held while Jess was trying to push. "So, either you're coming out, or I'm coming in." And taking the big risk if she did.

As it turned out, she went in. It seemed the only expedient thing to do when a low rumble of distant thunder threatened the approach of yet another storm front. Thankfully, it hadn't startled the horse, but Julie wasn't about to get this close only to have the beast run when the next clap of thunder got a little closer. So she plowed straight into the thicket of bushes, kept her head down, batted away avenging branches trying to scratch her face, stepped on more squishy things than she could even imagine and didn't stop until she was standing almost face to face with the horse, who instantly became more interested in the sugar than anything else. "I trust you're going to make this easy on me," she said, when Fugitive gently licked what was left of the sugar in her hand. "At least easier than Jess will. Too bad a couple of sugar cubes won't do the trick with him."

In response the horse turned up her lips and whinnied.

"Okay, so maybe a couple more cubes. Is that what you want?" She pulled them from her pocket and held them up. After Fugitive had licked them from Julie's hand, she gave the horse a hug, then slipped a rope around her neck at the same time and tightened it. Then, like she was leading a horse on an everyday walk around the paddock, she led Fugitive straight to the trailer, no fuss, no muss, where Jess took over and got the filly inside. "Good girl," she said, once the horse was safe and comfy.

"I'm impressed," Jess said a few minutes later, once the trailer gate was safely latched.

"And I'm exhausted. All I want to do is go back to the stable, find a quiet corner and go to sleep."

"How about a nice, soft bed in a moderately comfortable cabin in the woods? Might not have all the same charm as a bale of straw in a stable, but it's closer than your house, meaning you'll be asleep a full fifteen minutes earlier there than if you go all the way home."

"Don't tempt me," she said, leaning back against the side of the truck, wondering if she had enough energy to make it to the passenger's door.

"You know you shouldn't have come out here by yourself," he said, stepping closer to her, putting his arms around her, pulling her into his chest.

She savored his support, his strength. Needed it for a moment. Needed someone to hold her up physically and emotionally. "*You* know you shouldn't have been driving that truck, not with your foot getting worse the way it is."

"We do what we have to do," he said, settling into the embrace.

"Because that's who we are," she said, on a contented sigh.

"Because that's who we are," he repeated.

"What are we going to do, Jess? We make all these resolutions to stay out of each other's lives, to walk away, to stay detached, then look at us. First chance we get and here we are, doing everything we know she shouldn't be doing. So tell me. What are we going to do?"

"Hell if I know."

Her sentiments exactly. Right now, maybe in the long run. She didn't know, didn't particularly care. At the moment she was in Jess's arms. That's all that mattered. One moment. "Well, since neither of us knows, how about for starters we hurry and get this horse back to the stables? Then get out of our wet clothes."

"And by getting out of our wet clothes, you would mean…?"

She laughed. "One step at a time, Jess. Moment to moment. That's the *only* thing I can mean right now. No promises, no plans. That's the deal." It sounded calculating, but that was the only way she could do this. Because if Jess knew that her proposed deal was wrapped so tightly around her heart it hurt, everything would change. She wasn't sure how, but she was pretty sure she didn't want to know yet. Especially since there was so much to work out between them, so many complications and doubts. So much to confront, or avoid. The proverbial elephant in the room. And their elephant seemed bigger than most.

An elephant she was perfectly willing to avoid for a while. Moment to moment...not perfect, but good enough.

"Should we shake on it?" he asked, grabbing hold of Julie and pulling her back into his arms.

"I think this is way better, deal or no deal," she murmured, unable to resist reaching up to press her lips to his. Familiar, firm... The kiss started with passion, no building up to it, nothing tentative. It was the kiss she knew from him, the one that turned her knees to jelly and sucked away every last ounce of self-control she wanted to pretend she had. The remembered taste of him... she'd dreamed about it, yearned over it through the years. Never been able to get past a first kiss with anyone else because the first kiss with Jess had been everything. And now, as tongues touched, and probed, and she felt his hard erection pressed to her pelvis, this was the dream playing out in reality, the only thing she'd ever wanted, ever needed... "Jess," she murmured, ready to give herself over right there. "Do you think we should...?"

At that moment, his cell phone jingled, and his immediate reaction was to pull it from his pocket to silence it. But she stopped him… "It might be someone wondering where we are. I think we need to let them know we've got Fugitive and we'll be back in a few minutes."

"Not the way I wanted this moment to end." He stepped back, cleared his throat and looked at the number calling him. "It's Bobby Lee," he said, clicking on. "Hey, I tried calling you a few minutes ago to let you know—"

Jess stopped in mid-sentence, listened, then gasped, "Where, exactly?"

"What is it?" Julie whispered.

Jess's reaction was a frown. "Look, don't move. I'm on my way. Do you understand me, Bobby Lee? *Do not move.* You're going to be fine, and we're going to get you out of there, but be very careful." He handed the phone to Julie. "He's injured. We've got to go find him. He's not sure where he is. Thinks he took a wrong turn on the shortcut. Don't have any more details because he was fighting just to be coherent. I think he's probably slipping in and out of consciousness. Also, I don't have any medical supplies with me, so call Rafe or Rick and get help. Tell them where we are right now, have them call Will to get a search and rescue started, and the police department as well. We need everybody on this we can find, as fast as possible."

Without missing a beat, Julie made the necessary phone calls while Jess gathered up the few items they had available to them, items taken from the back of the truck—rope, flashlight, blanket, shovel and extra rain slickers. His cane, a reminder to both of them how difficult this was going to be. And this time no arguments. She wasn't going to let Jess put himself at risk. She needed him too much… "Bobby Lee's not answering now," Julie said, grabbing the rope, blanket and shovel from him.

"I'm not surprised. I think he's pretty critical." He pointed to the path about two hundred feet off from where the truck was parked. "And I think that's where we have to start our search since that's where the shortcut comes out."

"You can't do the hike, Jess. I'm serious. Driving is one thing. But this is dangerous, and…and you're going to hold me back. I can't wait for you."

"Who's the one taking the risk?" he asked her as he headed off to cross that span between the truck and where the search would officially start. "Because going out there, alone, isn't smart. Goes against all the rules."

She laughed. "Well, then, I've just changed the rules. Also, I suppose that officially makes us quite the pair, doesn't it, since you change the rules all the time, too?" She gave Jess a quick kiss on the cheek and he slipped her the flashlight. "Stay on the path. I don't want to have to come looking for you, too."

"Be careful," he said, as she turned and ran off into the woods.

"You, too," she called back. She didn't like leaving him behind that way. Probably didn't like it as much as he didn't like being left behind, but there wasn't anything else she could do here. Bobby Lee needed help, and someone had to respond. Tonight she was that someone.

Just like Jess, she said to herself as she headed down the path. Maybe that's when she understood…truly understand the nature of the man she loved.

The admission of what she'd known in her heart all along stopped her in her tracks. She did love him. Had never stopped loving him. She smiled to herself, and kept moving forward. "Just like Jess." This time, being alike didn't scare her. In fact, it was all she wanted to be.

"Where is she?" Rafe asked, running up to his brother's side.

"About ten minutes ahead of me. Couldn't stop her." Actually, he was proud of Julie. Sure, he didn't like the idea of her being out there alone, but she was…Julie Clark. And that said it all.

"Well, Rick is taking the trail from the other way in, and he's got Will with him. Will's got the call out for as many volunteers as we can find, Edie's gone down to the stable to coordinate the effort, so we'll be at full strength in about twenty minutes."

"Edie?"

"She may be ready to deliver any minute now, but there's no way anybody's going to keep her out of the action. You know how she is…strong. Like Julie. Something we have in common, loving strong women." As the brothers walked the trail, shoulder to shoulder, Rafe flashed his light back and forth, illuminating everything in a wide swath in front of them.

"Like I keep telling you, you got lucky, big brother."

"Don't I know that. So, tell me. When are you going to get that lucky? Or let me rephrase that. When are you going to quit being so stubborn and see you and Julie for what you are?"

"It's complicated." Jess paused for a moment, leaned on his cane to take the weight off his foot.

"You know you and your doctor are going to have a serious discussion about your lack of good judgment when it comes to following doctor's orders, don't you?"

"Get in line. I think Julie's got you beat on that one."

"Like I said, when are you going to get as lucky as I got? And don't go telling me it's complicated again, because that's just putting off the inevitable. You love her. That's all there is. The rest of it doesn't matter. I know they always tell you not to put the cart before the horse, but I think you should. Grab hold of Julie and hang on tight before you figure out the rest of the mess, instead of waiting until the mess is figured out before you grab hold of her. It's easier when you have two figuring it out together, and it's a whole lot more fun. Life's too short to wait. So, don't."

"Easy for you to say," Jess snapped, taking up the march again.

"I was there, Jess. Same old man, same conflicts. The thing is, if you mess this up with Julie, if you walk away from her again for *any* reason, he wins. The issues don't go away. Mine haven't. But having Edie there to help me… What I'm trying to tell you, little brother, is that if you wait for everything to be perfect before you make your move, if you wait for everything to uncomplicate itself, you're going to spend the rest of your life alone. Julie loves you now, and you love her now. That's *all* you need."

"Right. Blink my eyes and life gets better. That's not me, Rafe."

"Not me either. But guess what? It did get better. The old man didn't win in my life. I did."

He wanted to believe it could be that easy. Wanted to believe. To win. "Look, Rafe, don't let me hold you back. You can cover more distance without me, and I think we're in real trouble with Bobby Lee. You need to go on ahead." Pushing people away wasn't all that difficult, especially when you had the right motivation. With Rafe right now, it was for the good of the patient. With Julie, it was going to be for her own good. Had to be for her own good. And had to be soon. Because the two of them together…that was the one factor in all this he couldn't control. When the two of them got together there was no control. "I'll be fine hanging back."

Rafe patted his brother on the shoulder. "Okay, I'll let you get away with putting it off. *For now.* But think about what I said. I resisted the whole thing with Edie because I thought I was too much like the old man to marry and have a good life. He damaged us, Jess. Nobody should ever have to go through what we did, but we survived it. And the thing is, Edie makes it better for me. There was no way I ever thought it could happen, thought that someone could help me put the past behind me and give me so much to look forward to in my future. But Edie does it for me, every day, every minute, little brother. Julie will do the same for you, when you finally decide to let her." With that, he went ahead of Jess, which was fine, because as Jess was bringing up the rear in this search, thinking about a future with

Julie was all he had on his mind. Last time he'd given it as serious a consideration as he'd been able to, he'd been a kid, and he'd come to the same conclusion then, too. Life with Julie was better in every aspect. Back then, though, the complications hadn't seemed so…difficult. But back then, in spite of everything his old man had put him through, his view on life with Julie had been idealistic. Marry her, be happy.

Now he had to concentrate on getting that stupid idealism out of his head. Or try figuring out what to do with it if he couldn't.

"I'm dialing my cell phone every minute or so," Julie told Rafe, who'd caught up to her. "So, how's Jess? I didn't like leaving him behind, but…"

"Limping along. Wrenching the hell out of his foot with every step. Headed for a couple weeks of bed rest at the least. Surgery at the most. But okay, otherwise."

She chuckled. "It's hard to keep him down, isn't it? But that's Jess. We can't expect him to be, or do, otherwise."

"Which is what always gets him in trouble." Rafe flashed the light ahead of him, and let his beam come to rest on Rick, who was approaching from the opposite direction.

"Darn," Julie muttered under her breath. They'd covered the whole shortcut now, and nobody had found Bobby Lee. "So, it looks like we go off trail," she said, doing a mental assessment of just how spread out this search was about to become.

"Well, I'm going back out to the trail head and lay out a search grid," Will said. "I've got at least thirty people who've checked in with Edie, and she's holding them, waiting for me to clear them to come out and start looking. I didn't want to do that if there was any chance we'd find him on the path."

"So I think the three of us should split up and cover as much of the area as possible before everybody else gets here, because that's when it's going to get crazy. Lots of people, lots of noise..." It was necessary, she knew that. The more people looking for Bobby Lee, the better his chances of being found and helped. But people obliterated tracks, drowned out subtle moans. In other words, the bad with the good. She wanted these next ten minutes to herself and, without another word to Rafe and Rick she headed back in the direction from which she'd come.

"Do you know how much she's like your brother?" Rick asked Rafe after they'd noticed that she'd left them behind.

"Having one of Jess in the family can be pretty exasperating at times. Not sure what I'm going to do with two of them."

"You think that's what's going to happen?" Rick asked.

Rafe nodded. "I'm pretty sure. As soon as Jess comes to his senses."

"Bobby Lee!" Jess shouted. His pace had slowed even more. He was off trail now, since there was no point in following the same trail both Julie and Rafe had taken before him. "Can you hear me, Bobby Lee?"

He wanted to hear something, but the only thing that responded to him was the distant thundering echo of yet another storm front moving in. Which could sign Bobby Lee's death warrant if they didn't get to him first. "Come on, Bobby! Answer me!"

He paused, listened. Heard...nothing at all

damn it! Not one damned thing. And so it went for another few minutes, calling, not being answered. Worrying about the storm, about Bobby Lee's condition, about his own condition as far as Julie was concerned. It was all a frustrating jumble, complicated by the fact that his foot was giving out. Even if he were to find Bobby Lee now, there was no way he was going to make it out of these woods on his own. In fact, he was about done. It was time to admit that if he went any farther, he was going to cause himself permanent damage.

And if he didn't go any further with Julie, that would be the worst damage of all. Fight her off as he might, Rafe was right about one thing. It was time to win. Otherwise he'd spend the rest of his life going around in the same circles he'd gone in up until now, never finding what he was looking for. But how the hell could he do it and not make a mess of it? That was the question that plagued him over and over.

And the guilt over Donna… "Damn," he muttered as the rain started to pick up again. He'd loved her, but not enough. He'd wanted to love her more, tried to love her more. But it wouldn't have ever been enough because she'd expected things from him that he couldn't be. And all the love in the world couldn't have forced the changes in him that he'd have needed to be with her. Bottom line...they'd been wrong for each other, and nothing about that could have been overcome. She'd wanted him in a way he could never be, and he'd wanted her in a way that she could never be.

But that look on her face... He could still see it, even now, when he shut his eyes and slid to the muddy ground underneath a pine tree to wait out the rescue. It was still there. That look. But only for a moment. Then all he could see was Julie. And instead of feeling his usual nothing, he felt...everything.

CHAPTER ELEVEN

JESS snapped his eyes open as words from an old tune jolted him out of his momentary slump. "Bobby Lee?" he called, pushing himself to his feet. He was around here. That had to be Julie's phone ringing. Somebody was calling Bobby Lee!

"Where are you?" he called out, turning on his flashlight.

"Jess?"

"Julie?"

"I heard your phone ring." He hobbled away from the tree, now barely able to put weight down on his foot. "It's close." The tune played again, and Jess couldn't help but smile. Rafe was right. Life with Julie was better. Even in the little jingle of an inconsequential song.

"Are you okay?" Julie asked, running up to his side.

"Trying to be." More than that, wanting to be.

She immediately put a steadying arm around his waist as she hit redial, and listened for her ring tone. "Over there," she said, pointing to an area just off to the right.

Which was exactly where they found Bobby Lee. On the ground, in the mud. Unconscious. A tree had crashed down on him and he was crushed underneath it, his slight body barely visible in the damage. Finding him anywhere in the storm was an amazing feat. Finding him there was a miracle.

"Pulse weak," Julie said, taking her first assessment. She looked up at Jess. "But it's not good. Thready, irregular. Maybe indicating internal hemorrhage."

"We've got him," Jess said on his phone. "Look, Rafe. I'm guessing crushed pelvis. Legs, too. Probably some internal injuries, maybe bleeding, considering the size of the tree that's got him down. Have the O.R. on standby, because he's not going to be stable enough to transfer someplace else when we get him in." If ever there had been a time they needed a full-out trauma unit, this was it. "Remind me to work faster on those trauma plans when we get back," he told Julie, sliding down to the ground next to Julie. "And kick me if you don't think I'm making it my top priority."

"Does that mean you're going to be hanging around Lilly Lake for a while?" she asked, wiggling down to her stomach to get a better look at Bobby Lee's situation.

"Maybe. I've been giving it some thought."

She glanced up briefly, water dripping off her rain hat in a steady stream. "Really? How hard can I kick you?"

"As hard as you want." Jess scooted in the direction of Bobby Lee's head. "Toss me your flashlight, will you?"

She did. "And how often can I kick you? Not that I intend to, but just in case…"

He flashed the light into Bobby Lee's eyes, letting out a sigh of relief when he saw exactly what he wanted to see. "Equal and reactive." A very good sign, meaning that if they were lucky, he didn't have substantial neurological damage. "Oh, and kick me as often as I need it. For the rest of my life, if you have to."

She looked over at him for a moment, studied his face, but didn't comment. "Bobby Lee, it's Julie. You're going to be fine," she said after a long pause. She was trying to position herself now to press a hand underneath the log in order to see what kind of bleeding she might be missing in the rain, in the mud, in the dark. "Jess and I are going to get you out of here in a couple of minutes, so just stay with us, okay? Listen to my voice…concentrate on it." Her hand pulled back slippery, and a quick sniff revealed the distinct coppery smell. Somewhere under there was an open wound. "Um, Jess…I think we should try and dig in around him, but only enough for better access since I think he could be crushed." They needed to get an IV in him as soon as someone brought it down the trail. Needed to get a pressure bandage on the open wound. Needed a better way to access and evaluate for more injuries. "Also, we're dealing with what I think could be a substantial open wound. I'm feeling a lot of bleeding." She pulled back, flashed the light under there again, couldn't see it.

Jess raised up. "Where?"

"Mid-abdomen I think. Didn't feel a puncture, but…"

No more words were spoken between them. Jess shot to his feet, then stepped over the tree.

Within a second he was digging with his hands, trying to free as much of Bobby as possible, without causing more damage. Julie was doing the same on her side, frantically scooping away the mud, fighting off the increasing wind, the increasing rain.

"We may have to get him out, risks and all," Jess shouted at her, as a bolt of lightning split the sky. "See what we can get immobilized. Hope he's not bleeding internally. Because with the way it's coming down now..." He glanced up as a loud crack somewhere overhead forewarned what he feared most. "Julie!" he screamed, shoving himself forward to cover as much of Bobby Lee's face as he could.

But too late. The top of a tall pine tree came crashing down on them, trunk, branches, needles, and he felt the thunk of it on his back, his legs. Felt the prick of the needles instantly shooting into skin like tiny darts. Felt...woozy. "Julie," he murmured. "Can you hear me? Julie..."

No answer. And the thoughts that went through his head... *Not again!* She couldn't be...she wasn't... No! "Come on, Julie," he choked, trying to get through the impossible clump of vegetation that fought to keep him pinned down in the mud. "Stay with me. Just…stay with me."

Blindly, frantically, he reached out as far as he could, tried to feel her. "Come on, sweetheart. Just grab my hand and hang on." Yet nothing… except the rain and the wind. And the racking pain shooting up his leg that threatened to drag him down into the slumbering abyss with Bobby Lee and Julie.

They were not visible now. None of the three of them. Totally covered. No one would hear them. No one would find them tonight. No one…

Jess's eyes began to droop. He recognized the signs of exhaustion mixed with pain. Felt the arms of Morpheus wrapping around him, lulling him to give in, promising him a place where the pain would subside for a while. But… "Julie," he mumbled, as she drifted into his thoughts, "Julie…" His salvation…the only thought on his mind as his eyes closed all the way.

Julie. Beautiful Julie…a nice face to drift off with. The only face he'd ever wanted to drift off with. Julie… Suddenly, his eyes shot back open. Where was she? He had to find her. That was the single thought that propelled the rescuer in him to take over, to fight off the pain threatening to drag him under. It's what he did, who he was. Who Julie needed. So with no clear way to accomplish anything, he struggled to roll over onto his side, hoping that somehow the shift in position would enable him to get to either Julie or move away from Bobby Lee enough to be able to help him. Turning slowly, trying not to put any pressure on his foot, he felt the stings of the cuts and scrapes from the tree on his face, his hands. Felt the burn of what he knew would require surgery and God only knew how much rehab slithering up his leg. But he found Bobby Lee's pulse, didn't note any appreciable change in it, thank God. "Julie," he yelled again, trying to push himself just a little farther in the direction where he knew she had to be. Still nothing from her, though, and he was frantic.

So now it was decision time. He could do whatever he could to take care of Bobby Lee or keep trying to find Julie. His heart wanted Julie. But he couldn't leave Bobby Lee alone.

Then it struck him. He had one chance…the only chance he'd have until help arrived. One that might, and probably would, end his risk-taking days. But it didn't matter. Nothing did, except Julie. So, gritting his teeth to what he knew would be coming, Jess rolled all the way over on his back and kicked up at the branches covering him, hoping he'd have enough strength left in his legs to do this. Adrenalin strength, as it turned out. Screaming at the top of his lungs to summon it up, he kicked the treetop up just enough to give him time to squirm up out of the mud and push it off to the side. It wasn't much of a kick even with the adrenalin, wasn't much of a push either, thanks to what was now a broken foot, but it gave him room…just enough room to crawl out from under the copious branches and needles then turn around and pull at the treetop, move it enough to get it all the way off Bobby Lee. And that's when he found her… Julie. Unconscious. Her face half submerged in the mud. But breathing. And with a strong pulse. "You'll keep," he whispered, brushing a twig from her hair after he'd done a fast assessment. "Bobby won't, though. But I'm not leaving you, Julie. I promise, I'm not leaving you."

In that moment, his doubts seemed trivial. His fears seemed unimportant. Whatever concern had been rattling around in him all this time vanished because Julie was all that mattered. The rest of it…he didn't give a damn anymore. Just simply didn't give a damn. He loved Julie Clark, always had, always would. Now it was time to make everything they'd done wrong right. How would Julie feel about that? Well, he wasn't sure. But she'd been the one to kiss him first last time they'd kissed. That counted for something. Hopefully, it counted for everything because Julie *had* kissed him.

"He's fine," Rafe said, dropping down into the chair across the room from his brother. "Bobby Lee is stable. His injuries are significant, some broken bones, that gash in his belly, a moderate concussion, no internal damages, though. So we got lucky there, and he's probably going to be ready to transfer to a rehab center in a couple of days. And Sleeping Beauty here…" He nodded at Jess. "Not too bad, considering how it could have turned out."

"I'm awake," Jess said, still too groggy from the anesthesia to open his eyes. "So, how *did* it turn out?"

"For you it was a torn ligament, ruptured tendon, cracked talus, a couple of broken metatarsals, specifically the second and third. Oh, and a dislocation of distal phalanx of your big toe. All repaired. So the good news is you had a brilliant surgeon on the job," Julie said from the bed next to Jess, where she'd been resting since she'd been admitted with a moderate concussion. No other injuries. "The bad news is you've got at least three months ahead of you where you're going to be off your foot, come hell or high water. With a pretty stern nurse who isn't going to put up with your bad behavior. And there's going to be physical therapy with that."

Jess groaned. "I don't need physical therapy, unless…" He attempted his usual, albeit lopsided-for-the-moment grin. "How do you define physical therapy?"

"You can't even open your eyes yet, and listen to you, already giving me trouble."

Rafe chuckled. "If I weren't so tired, I'd leave you two in private. But there's nothing in me that's going to get me out of this chair for the next hour. So, Julie, do what you have to with Jess. You have my permission to tie him down to the bed, if that's what…" His voice drifted off, and Rafe was dead to the world.

"You heard what your brother said," Julie said, pushing herself out of bed. She was washed clean of all mud now, and comfortable in a set of surgical scrubs. Her head ached, her muscles were sore, but she was comfortable because Jess was there. "He gave me permission to tie you to the bed. But would it be okay if I just crawled in next to you and held you down instead?"

"How long has that been your ring tone?" Jess asked, his question totally unexpected.

"I'm not sure what you mean," she lied.

He opened one eye to look at her. "Sure you do. Something about Jessie's girl? You know, from that old 1980s song." He hummed a bit of the tune in a very ragged way, then opened one droopy eye and looked at her. "Tell me, Julie."

"Okay, I've had it as long as I've had the phone. A couple of years. Had it on the phone before this, and the one before that."

"And…?"

"And in my mind I changed the lyrics a little to *being Jess's girl*. Now you know all my deep, dark secrets. Are you happy?"

Jess finally opened both his eyes. "Very happy. Would it be okay if you crawled in next to me *every night* for the rest of your life? I made the offer before…letting you kick me for the rest of your life."

"That was an offer?" she asked.

"Thought it was a pretty good offer."

"Well, as offers go, I guess it was, considering that it was an offer à la Jess. But we still have some things to work out," she warned him. She knew he wasn't over Donna yet, wasn't over the pain he felt because of her death, or the guilt of pushing her away. But he wouldn't be working it out alone now, because Jess wasn't alone. Intellectually, he was coming to terms with what that meant. More than that, he was feeling it emotionally. And in those moments when he didn't…she did have permission to kick him. But a gentle, loving kick, and only from her heart to his.

"Old news. I love you, you said yourself that you want to be Jess's girl… Oh, and out there in the woods, when I thought I'd lost you…" The deep breath he drew in was ragged. "I never felt that emptiness with you, Julie. The only time in my life when I didn't feel empty was when you were making me feel…alive."

"We let too much get in the way of what's important," she said, crawling in next to him, lying on her side to snuggle. "When we were kids, it couldn't be helped. Everything was going against us and we weren't smart enough to figure it out. But we're not kids anymore, Jess. We get a second chance, and it's got to be the one that counts. *If you want it to count.*"

"Do you?"

"I've always loved you, if that means anything. I think that's why I always wanted to come back to Lilly Lake. Even if I couldn't have you, you were here in so many ways. I was willing to let that be enough. But it's not, Jess. I do want to be Jess's girl. More than that, I want Jess to be the man he is. No changes necessary. If you decide you want to give up medicine and firefighting and raise alpacas, I'm with you. Or if you want to spend your days doing watercolor landscapes, I'll be the one holding your palette. Our life, Jess, isn't going to come with some preconceived plans. We'll find our way as we need to find it, and the rest of it we'll work on when we have to."

"In other words, keeping it simple?"

"In other words, keeping it *us*. We lost that chance once, but there's no one there to stop us now."

"No one," Rafe mumbled from his chair. "So kiss her, will you, Jess? So I can get some sleep."

"Brother knows best," Jess said, pulling Julie into his arms.

"So, that's the deal. I'll run the trauma department as a physician. But I'm also going to work with the fire department in the capacity of the new director of paramedic training services," Jess said. "And I'll be going out on runs, because I still like being there to make the first assessment. Best of both worlds. Although my firefighting days may be limited for a while." He held up his cane.

"Best of *neither* world yet," Julie reminded him. "One more month, *or longer,* on the cane, not negotiable." She put down the horse brush and walked over to Jess, who was sitting in front of the stall where the newest love of his life, a horse named Julie, was nuzzling him from behind.

"You have such a way with the ladies," she said, bending down to kiss him.

"I have such a way with the Julies," he corrected.

"Strong redheads," she said.

He smiled. "Well you've got to give me credit for one thing...I've had plenty of time to finish the plans for the trauma department expansion these past few weeks. I turned them over to the architect a few days ago, and started working on something else. More expansion, actually." He held out a sketch pad. "Take a look, add your notes, make suggestions."

Julie frowned skeptically. "We can't knock out another wall, Jess. The rest of the space is promised to Pediatrics. Rick's got some ideas, and you know he's trying to get Summer Adair to come on full time as head nurse in the unit."

"Well, Pediatrics could be included."

She took the pad, opened it, looked at the first page, and a smile spread over her face. "Really?"

"The big old oak tree won't be touched either. It will be the centerpiece of our front yard and I expect to sit underneath it with the prettiest girl in the world for the rest of our lives."

Their place. Their house.

"It's permanent, Jess. Are you sure that's really what you want? Permanent roots in Lilly Lake? I know we said we'd stay here for now, but...will this be enough for you?"

"It will be everything because it's what we've always wanted." The dream that had begun when they had been teenagers, and was finally coming true. "It's time, Julie. Seventeen years is a long time to wait, so it's time to start again, and get it right."

Julie sat down on the bench next to Jess, and settled in perfectly when he pulled her into his arms. "My thoughts exactly, because I want to marry you, Jess Corbett, and have lots of babies with you."

"And lots of horses."

"Absolutely. For the next seventy or eighty years," she said, sighing the sigh of a very happy woman.

"What about the risk-taking thing?"

"I'm okay with it. Got myself used to the idea, as long as you promise not to be too casual about it. And to listen to the people who love you when we tell you we're worried."

Jess chuckled. "I'm not talking about the risks I take. I'm talking about the risks you take. Not sure I want the woman I love to be out there in the way of harm the way you seem to like being."

"Oh, so when the shoe is on the other foot, the fit isn't quite so good."

"I have a right to worry."

"So do I," she quipped. "And maybe, now that you know how it feels to be on the other end, you won't be quite so…well, I don't want to call it careless, because you're not careless. Maybe the word I want here is unmindful…unmindful of how much you're loved. And by some loved more than anybody else in the world."

"Believe me, I have a lot to be mindful of," he whispered, nuzzling her ear.

"So do I," Julie said, looking down the stall row at all the horses, and all the volunteers scurrying to take care of them. "Do you think Grace would have expected this…expected *us?*"

"I think it was always part of Aunt Grace's plan. She had this uncanny way of knowing when nobody else did. So I have this hunch that she knew you were the one for me the first time she ever laid eyes on you. Like I did, the first time

I ever laid eyes on you. I think that's what she meant when she told me I wasn't taking advantage of the things I had in life. That I had more to give. That I was underestimating myself. She meant that about you, Julie. She knew we'd find each other again."

"And we did."

"Julie!" Summer shouted from the opposite end of the stable. "Got a horse on the loose, halfway over to Jasper. Probably a runaway. It's pretty beat up, malnourished, dehydrated. Still up on its feet, but the sheriff over there said we need to come get it right away because it's got a bad gash on its shoulder that needs treatment. Can you go take care of it?"

"On my way," she shouted back, then scooted off the bench and extended a hand to Jess. "Going with me?" she asked.

"For the rest of my life," he said, taking her hand. "Want me to drive?"

"Oh, yeah. Like I'm going to fall for that again. Last time you went against doctor's orders, this is what happened to you." She pointed to the cast on his foot. "This time, I may not be the doctor, but I have my own set of orders, and the answer to your question is..."

He hobbled up to Julie and pulled her into his arms, then kissed her hard. "And that's the answer to *my* question."

"Well, I think I like your answer better," Julie said, a contented smile sliding to her lips.

"Good, my love, because it's the same answer you'll be getting again, and again, and again..."

* * * * *

Mills & Boon® *Large Print* Medical

June

NEW DOC IN TOWN	Meredith Webber
ORPHAN UNDER THE CHRISTMAS TREE	Meredith Webber
THE NIGHT BEFORE CHRISTMAS	Alison Roberts
ONCE A GOOD GIRL…	Wendy S. Marcus
SURGEON IN A WEDDING DRESS	Sue MacKay
THE BOY WHO MADE THEM LOVE AGAIN	Scarlet Wilson

July

THE BOSS SHE CAN'T RESIST	Lucy Clark
HEART SURGEON, HERO…HUSBAND?	Susan Carlisle
DR LANGLEY: PROTECTOR OR PLAYBOY?	Joanna Neil
DAREDEVIL AND DR KATE	Leah Martyn
SPRING PROPOSAL IN SWALLOWBROOK	Abigail Gordon
DOCTOR'S GUIDE TO DATING IN THE JUNGLE	Tina Beckett

August

SYDNEY HARBOUR HOSPITAL: LILY'S SCANDAL	Marion Lennox
SYDNEY HARBOUR HOSPITAL: ZOE'S BABY	Alison Roberts
GINA'S LITTLE SECRET	Jennifer Taylor
TAMING THE LONE DOC'S HEART	Lucy Clark
THE RUNAWAY NURSE	Dianne Drake
THE BABY WHO SAVED DR CYNICAL	Connie Cox